Comfortable Graves

by
Roy LeBlanc

© 2014 Roy LeBlanc

All Rights Reserved.

No part of this publication may be reproduced, stored in a retrieval system, or transmitted, in any form or by any means, electronic, mechanical, photocopying, recording, or otherwise, without the written permission of the author.

ISBN: 978-0-578-67558-9

This book is printed on acid-free paper.

Printed in the United States of America

This book is a work of fiction. Names, characters, places, and incidents either are the products of the author's imagination or are used fictitiously. Any resemblance to actual events or locales or persons, living or dead, is entirely coincidental.

FOREWORD

My introduction to Roy LeBlanc's writing is his most recent book "Comfortable Graves". I was captivated from the very beginning by the small town setting and how Poplar Grove's sense of community was manipulated by corrupt politicians, sexual deviance, racist hate, and murder. The book captivates the reader's attention because lines of right and wrong are continually crossed by narcissistic personalities. The author's creation of these dysfunctional characters that misuse political office and are corrupted by racist hate is fascinating.

A white mob stormed the small town courthouse in the dark of night to serve as judge, jury, and executioners of an African American man without any regard to trial or truth. Most despicable was their keeping of mementos from the lynching which served as trophies confirming their hatred. In the end there is satisfaction and redemption correcting these wrongs.

As Mayor and resident of a small city similar to Poplar Grove, I admit the book lured me in from the beginning. I share in title only the role of Mayor with one of the book's pivotal characters, Spencer. Thankfully, I am in possession of a moral compass and have learned to embrace differences. People can change and I know that when the power of education connects with the heart's ability to love then forgiveness becomes possible. The significance of this book dares to take on difficult societal issues of our day but leaves hope that even when imperfect, we can make a difference.

Bradley Necaise
Mayor
Poplarville, MS

1

REMEMBER THE *CHOOSE YOUR OWN* *Adventure* readers? They were adventure books like *The Hardy Boys* and *Nancy Drew,* but these offered options as the plot developed. Do you stop or go? Ride a bike or walk? Stay indoors or out? Do you approach the person of your dreams? Should you stay with the same friends you have known forever or learn new things from intriguing strangers? Do you stay in the same comfortable neighborhood or risk moving to a new town? Every combination of choices the reader selects leads to different and unpredictable outcomes in the chapters ahead. The story's plot always unfolds differently with each reading and each decision the reader makes.

Andre and Clarence read the books repeatedly, making different choices each time, trying over and over to create the perfect ending. Frustrated, they often tried to cheat the books, taking a shortcut by reading the final chapters first. Identifying the ideal ending in hindsight was easy. Getting to it, however, was nearly impossible. Even with the best intentions, things always got screwed up along the way.

Andre and Clarence had been friends forever, from fourth grade to high school to college. In fact, it was hard to remember any time they were not friends.

Enos was the meanest kid at Hynes elementary school. He was named after Enos Slaughter, the Yankee outfielder in the 1950s. Enos had a system for stealing lunch money. His classmates were all expected to deliver their twenty-five cents to him before the morning bell rang. Back then lunch and milk cost a quarter. Enos sat on the school's back steps, collecting quarters. Andre decided to make a stand and refused to turn over his money. "Lost it," he told him. But Enos saw Andre eating lunch and was waiting after school. He hit him hard. Andre fell to the ground.

"You owe me fifty cents tomorrow!" Enos said. He kneed Andre in the ribs for fun.

The next day Andre again refused to give him any money. "I'm going to beat the crap out of you." Andre understood that Enos would make an example of him but if he gave in, Enos would own him. Andre was not going to be a wimp. Enos raised his right fist behind his head to give his punch greater momentum. A new student stepped in front of Andre, blocking Enos.

"I don't like you very much." The new student was unafraid. He threw a right hook, a left hook, then a right uppercut. Enos was on the ground. His nose was broken and his jaw was wired shut for two months. He ate lunch through a straw.

"I'm Clarence. This is my first day at Hynes," he said with a big silly smile.

"I'm Andre. Nice to meet you." From that day forward Andre knew he could count on his new friend.

They grew up during a time when New Orleans was a remarkable place, rich in history and tolerance. It was a city where they felt safe and comfortable in their blue-collar neighborhoods with strong families. Desegregated public swimming pools were a popular escape from the intense heat and July humidity, although segregation was never a real issue since light-skinned, blue-eyed creoles like Clarence could easily pass for white. The lifeguards tried to keep boys and girls separated, but their inadequate efforts were no match for Clarence. Once he realized that everyone basically had the same objectives, he became unstoppable.

Andre remembered the day Clarence figured it all out. They were walking home from Hynes School and came across a porn magazine discarded in a drainage ditch. Clarence opened it to a random page and stopped; he had a puzzled look with one eyebrow raised and a big smile. "Andre, do you think they want it as much as we do?" he asked, pointing out a photo of a woman enjoying sex. "They must! They must!" he said, while enthusiastically showing Andre additional magazine photos proving his point.

The first time Clarence held a girl's hand, he fell hard for her. He thought he had found true love until she had sex with some neighborhood boys she invited into her bedroom. "I don't understand what you are upset about. We're not married!" Clarence was devastated. But Andre predicted there would be more girls, and there were, many more.

As young teenagers one episode was most memorable. "I need you, buddy! Come quick!" Clarence said in a panicked tone. Andre drove the two blocks to Clarence's house and parked in his driveway. The carport was on the right side below a bathroom window. The front door was open. Clarence climbed out the bathroom window and jumped onto the carpet roof.

"Keep the car running!"

Clarence ran across the carport roof and leaped to the ground. "Let's go! Let's go!"

Denise was a girl in the neighborhood. Her father happened to read her diary. He kicked Clarence's front door in and was going from room to room looking for him. They were blocks away but could still see the angry dad on foot running after them.

"You little bastard. Come back here!"

Clarence suggested they go back and chase him around a little for kicks. He was always willing to do anything for love.

Three beautiful girls struck up a conversation with Clarence and Andre one Saturday afternoon in the French Quarter. Eventually the girls invited them to a cookout and party the next weekend. The tallest girl wrote the address and her number on Clarence's arm with red lipstick. The party was not at their house. It was at the "Walking Man's Friend," a run-down used car lot on Canal Street, and it wasn't a cookout. It was a hot dog boil! Andre smelled a rat. "It's a setup. Those girls work for this car lot," he explained to Clarence. "They're paid bird-dog fees for everyone that shows up." Clarence insisted on going anyway.

The salesman convinced Clarence to buy a 650-dollar Mercury, as-is with no warranty. "Look, the taillights work! Ain't that something!" the salesman said. The car broke down before they got it home. The tow bill was $75 but Clarence was not angry. He was smiling.

"You rascal! You screwed that girl, didn't you?"

Clarence did not answer Andre, but he kept smiling.

Eventually Clarence earned an associate degree in general studies from Delgado Community College. He was extremely smart, but not in the limited ways recognized by traditional classroom education. Over the years Clarence always found a way to make a good living.

He purchased two old shotgun homes in the Tremé neighborhood. They were both condemned and scheduled to be demolished by the city. Clarence dismantled the homes himself and sold most of the valuable antique architectural features. He kept the old cypress frame lumber and used it to make antique-type furniture. The tables, chairs, and desks sold well in various tourist shops on Magazine Street. He sold the two vacant lots to real-estate investors.

Andre finished second in his class at Tulane Law and became a lead litigator with Jones, Adams and Dunbar. His firm was one of the largest in New Orleans, with eighty attorneys on staff. He specialized in campaigns, elections, and politics. Some of Andre's time was spent making sure Louisiana elections were honest and above board. That was a real oxymoron—honest Louisiana elections.

The truth was, Andre was hired by elected officials trying to make life difficult and expensive for opposing candidates. Lawsuits challenging residency and campaign finance reporting would most likely scare away all but the most determined. He also enjoyed defense work. When a former governor's wife accepted two hundred thousand dollars from a Japanese businessman, Andre handled the defense. He convinced a jury that the governor had no knowledge of the cash transaction. "If another man gives my wife a significant amount of cash, I want to know what is going on!" the US Attorney said in closing arguments. The governor said he would prefer not to know. The ten men on the jury laughed and smiled in agreement. Andre won.

Andre said he was always amazed at the political skullduggery that took place in this state. But he didn't complain because it was a very lucrative practice, and politicians always paid cash in advance. "No one accepts IOUs from Louisiana politicians," he said.

Clarence and Andre made a good team. Andre helped Clarence get through middle school, high school, and college. He wrote his college papers and did his geometry homework. He worked with him to keep passing grades. Good-natured Clarence, on the other hand, was always happy to protect Andre from bullies and defend him. Clarence was a lover and a fighter. He'd had Andre's back since fourth grade. It was a remarkable friendship.

2

SINCE USABLE LAND IN NEW Orleans was limited by swamps, marshes, and floods, everyone lived close together in ancient neighborhoods built on scarce higher ground. For generations New Orleanians had learned to get along, some more than others, explaining Clarence's mixed-race Creole heritage. "There was a lot of fence hopping going on back then," his grandmother used to say.

Things began to change once the interstate highways were finished and the commute to St. Tammany Parish became practical. New subdivisions were built across the "North Shore" of Lake Pontchartrain to accommodate those eager to leave New Orleans. New subdivisions required approved colors, gardens, and even types of acceptable grass. Everything looked exactly alike. Subdivision boards were made up of individuals who failed at student government in high school and viewed the neighborhood associations as redemption. The "white flight" gave up Audubon Park, streetcars, antebellum homes, the French Quarter, and the diversity of a culture-rich city for the cookie-cutter land of strip malls, vinyl siding, and annoying neighborhood governing boards.

This first "North Shore" exodus in the 1970s damaged the city's tax base; cutting "unnecessary expenses" like public swimming pools became a routine necessity. But it was the crack cocaine epidemic and its rampant waves of violent street crime that caused even people who loved the city, like Clarence, to finally consider leaving. With eleven generations of his family buried in New Orleans, Clarence found that moving was a hard decision. "It's always home," he said.

Mr. Dolese was over seventy years old and enjoyed sitting on his porch telling D-Day stories. He had been Clarence's neighbor for decades. Mr. Dolese was an avid gardener who meticulously maintained his lawn. He was working on his flower beds when approached by two drug-crazed thugs. They demanded money; Mr. Dolese had none. Then they demanded his wedding ring. "I haven't taken this ring off since the Truman administration," he said defiantly. The addicts pulled out a switchblade and cut off his finger. They calmly walked away, laughing. The New Orleans Police Department showed up thirty minutes later. They said it was another example of random street crime.

Clarence said he could handle a seventy-mile commute. The sixty-minute drive was a small price to pay for peace of mind and safety. It was time for something new, maybe even a job in a new town. He sat at his desk with a map and compass and drew a red circle representing a seventy-mile radius around New Orleans.

"What about Picayune, Mississippi, or Bogalusa, Louisiana?" he asked Andre while looking at the circle.

"Bogalusa is a paper mill town and has no interstate accessibility," Andre said. He reminded Clarence of the old joke about the girl who asked her boyfriend to kiss her where it stinks. So he drove her to Bogalusa. "The mill smells terrible, and the only way they make money is by selling beer." Since the adjacent Pearl River County in Mississippi across the Pearl River was dry, everyone came to Bogalusa to buy alcohol. "The convenience stores sell gas and beer, nothing else," Andre said. Clarence drew a red X over Bogalusa. Andre knew nothing about Picayune except that insurance companies had more losses from automobile fires there than any other American city of that size. "Do they just burn cars when the payments come due?" Clarence asked with a smile and wrote another red X.

They refilled their coffee cups. "Let me take a look at the map," Andre said. About sixty miles northeast of New Orleans and twenty minutes north of Picayune was Poplar Grove, Mississippi. It was right at the outer edge of his circle. Andre reminded Clarence about his visit there a few years before. The annual Blueberry Festival was one of the largest events in the area. Poplar Grove was quiet, safe, and slow paced. It was the perfect escape from big-city problems.

"They had blueberry ice cream, pie, jelly, preserves, syrup, and a cobbler-baking contest. Horses pulled hay-lined wagons for tours of the nearby vineyards. Main Street was closed to traffic, and the town's small commercial area became the festival center. Vendors came from all over selling folk art and crafts. Ice cream was made on a hundred-year-old John Deere gasoline-powered churn. Kettle corn and fried pig skin was prepared in the food area. A display of antique farm equipment was set up at the far end of Main Street. It is a slower pace. No one is in a hurry," Andre said.

The festival kicked off early with a 5K race and one-mile fun run/walk. The start and finish line was in front of the historic old Pearl River County Courthouse. The run wound its way along the oak-lined residential streets past many grand old homes, relics from Poplar Grove's prosperous past.

The town's economy had been based on lumber and, more recently, tung oil trees. The oil from the tung nuts had been used in paint and wood treatment for decades. However, in 1969 Hurricane Camille destroyed the trees. Oil-based paints were becoming obsolete anyhow, and no one bothered to replant. Blueberry farms replaced the tung oil trees.

The town of Enterprise, Alabama, had a monument honoring the boll weevil, which destroyed the town's cotton fields. Peanuts replaced cotton. Enterprise was now the prosperous peanut capital of the South. Poplar Grove hoped for a similar economic resurrection with blueberries, although no one suggested a monument to Hurricane Camille.

Poplar Grove's community college provided a degree of culture with a Shakespeare Dinner and three annual plays sponsored by the drama department. Ironically, *To Kill a Mockingbird* by Harper Lee was a favorite. The college strictly followed the county's prohibition regarding alcohol. A few years back some boys had a secret beer party in their dorm room. Carefully they bagged the empty cans and bottles, hiding all evidence in the trash. The frat boys were arrested the next evening after they were turned in by garbage men.

The college never faced enrollment trouble, since many LSU flunk-outs ended up here. No doubt their families hoped to get them back on the right alcohol-free track. Although the consumption of alcohol in Pearl River County was strictly prohibited, making money on it was not. Each year during Mardi Gras season, the sheriff's department erected "insurance checks" on roads heading south toward New Orleans. Drivers found with beer were charged with "illegal transportation of alcohol across county lines." The fine was 535 dollars or twenty-two days in the Pearl River County jail. Everyone paid the fine.

Also of interest to Clarence, Poplar Grove was known for upside-down pineapples. A series of investigative articles claimed the town had a large and secret swingers community, with spouse-swapping parties held the first Friday of each month. Host responsibilities rotated on a monthly basis among group members. The host couple provided food and music. The Swingers Club met in a secret basement of a building owned by a Poplar Grove private school. Each month the designated host couple shopped at the local Food Cougar grocery on a certain day at a specific time. The upside-down pineapple in their basket was code to other club members that the event would proceed as planned. Words were never spoken.

Three years ago Andree attended the Poplar Grove Blueberry Festival. He arrived early enough to compete in the 5K race, hoping that his age group would be small, making it easy to win a trophy. He parked a few blocks away and walked over to the courthouse. The morning was cool with a heavy mist. Civil War and Spanish-American War monuments in the town square were barely visible through the dampness.

The courthouse was the largest building in town, constructed of brick and stone. Andre loved old buildings and knew Clarence did as well. Neither of them had ever lived in a house that was not at least a century old. It was a New Orleans thing. Instead of warming up for the run, Andre sat on the peaceful stone steps and admired the southern charm of this beautiful town. Poplar Grove seemed perfect for Clarence, and Andre did everything possible to encourage him. "Surely you'll love this peaceful town," Andre said, placing a green check on Clarence's map.

There were troubling things about Poplar Grove Andre did not know, but later wished to God he had. In 1959, a white couple was driving on a county road between Lumberton and Poplar Grove when their car broke down. The man pushed the disabled Chevy to the road's shoulder and walked off searching for assistance. Allegedly during his absence the woman was tied up in the car's backseat and raped. A twenty-three-year-old black man named Mack Parker was accused. He was arrested and held in the courthouse jail. After a long interrogation by four police officers and no lawyers, Mack signed a written confession.

A few days before trial, a hooded mob abducted him from his cell after a "careless" deputy left the keys available. Mack's desperate screams were heard across Poplar Grove that night, but no one came to his assistance. "Help me! Help me! Please! I didn't do it! I didn't hurt no white lady!" He cried for his mother. Mack's desperate grip on the cell bars was torn free; he was dragged down the courthouse steps by his feet, knocking out his front teeth. They were picked up as souvenirs by members of the angry mob.

He was beaten without mercy and shot. Mack's mutilated body was dumped in the Pearl River. Those involved were well known in town, but FBI investigations resulted in no indictments. The local judge encouraged grand-jury members to preserve "our way of life." The Poplar Grove Council adopted a resolution calling the lynching "necessary and justifiable."

Similar resolutions were adopted by the Poplar Grove Retired Policemen Association, Teachers' Association, The Civic Good Government Association, The Lawyers' League, and the Regular Democratic

Association, among others. The FBI spent years on multiple investigations, but no one in Poplar Grove ever talked and no one was ever convicted. The old courthouse jail was now used to store Blueberry Festival equipment. There were no markers or monuments remembering these events. Unaware, Andre sat on those very courthouse steps waiting for a 5K race to begin.

3

OLD US HIGHWAY 11 ENDED at Power's Junction near Irish Bayou on the east side of New Orleans. It ran north, crossing Lake Pontchartrain with a 1930s bridge built during the administration of Governor Huey P. Long. The two-lane highway passed through Poplar Grove, eventually winding up in Chicago. Interstate I-10 ran parallel to the old road, which ran alongside the L&N railroad tracks. Depots and stations were established every ten miles along the tracks, eventually growing into towns. Poplar Grove was originally just another stop on the L&N Line. It now benefited from having its own I-10 interchange, with fast food and gas stations. Andre and Clarence drove the old road, looking forward to the relaxed pace of a slower time.

"Andre, I could enjoy this commute," Clarence said while pointing out old homes along the way. They arrived on time for an appointment at Poplar Grove's only real-estate agency.

The agent was an attractive middle-aged woman with a thin figure, blond hair pulled behind her ears, and a string of pearls around her neck. She was elegant in a Grace Kelly sort of way. Clarence stared into her blue eyes.

"I'm Lesley. My husband owns the Ford dealership in town," she said, handing them business cards. "He is also mayor of Poplar Grove," she added in a matter-of-fact way. Andre wasn't sure if she was a really good salesperson promoting her husband's business or just wanted to make sure Clarence understood she was married.

Andre recognized her husband's name, Spencer Barnes. He'd obtained a small degree of fame recently. Poplar Grove had a short-lived natural gas boom. Spencer drilled a few unsuccessful natural gas wells and stored the used drilling pipe on his property. He eventually donated the old pipe to the city of New Orleans. The city used it to support the aboveground electrical cables on the River Front streetcar line. Spencer was interviewed by local TV stations and the *Times-Picayune*. The mayor presented him with a golden key to the city in a special ceremony held at Gallier Hall. The award recognized "outstanding generosity," according to the mayor of New Orleans.

Somehow Spencer's drilling pipe had contracted a degree of radioactivity which went undetected. It was unnoticed until an environmental program at Tulane University detected unusual readings along the riverfront. They were testing for radioactivity from the Waterford III nuclear power plant north of New Orleans. Spencer claimed no knowledge of this, but monitoring and litigation were ongoing. The New Orleans mayor eventually revoked the golden key award.

Clarence waited for Lesley to extend her hand. A gentleman never offered his hand first. It was left to the lady to decide if she wanted to shake. She offered her hand. Clarence held her hand for a long time and then placed his left hand over hers. "I want you to know how much I appreciate your efforts," he said.

Andre notice splotches of redness appearing on her ivory white neck as she looked away. "Oh my!" she said in a wonderful southern drawl of elongated vowels while fanning her face with her left hand. Clarence discussed his price range and desired features. Andre looked at pictures of current real-estate listings and noticed her University of Southern Mississippi degree framed on the wall and her Junior League membership certificate naming her Social Chair.

Lesley took them to a nearby home recently listed. It was a 160-year-old large farmhouse near Main Street priced well within

Clarence's budget. All property here was inexpensive when compared to New Orleans. The one-acre property faced the courthouse and was landscaped with mature oaks and camellias. The home's exterior needed paint but was otherwise in good shape. On the inside every room was painted the same flat Navaho White. All the trim was painted the same color but in a gloss finish.

The kitchen sink had leaked for a very long time. The owner had tried to make repairs with duct tape, which blended in well with the gray countertops and actually looked presentable. Lesley said the owner replaced the tape anytime she was expecting guests. According to Lesley, the owner was also a championship grower of rare camellia varieties. That explained the beautiful and unusual blooms around the property.

Lesley said there was a small issue that required disclosure. She explained that the home was owned by Mrs. Misty Kate. "She was ninety-two years old and lived alone. She went to church each Sunday and Wednesday. Everyone loved her," Lesley said. "Mrs. Misty Kate died at home on a Thursday. Her body was not discovered until Sunday, when she failed to show for church." Clarence asked where exactly the body was for three days. "Right here," Lesley said, pointing to the stairs.

"Anything else we should know about this place?" Andre asked.

"Yes, there is one more thing," Lesley added. She explained that soldiers from the "Great War" were buried on the property as well. "When the Union army pulled out, two drunken Yankee soldiers lagged behind. An angry local mob forced them to dig their own graves, and shot them." Like many southerners Lesley referred to the Civil War as the Great War. Clarence asked where exactly the murdered soldiers were.

"Right under that oak," she said, pointing out the window.

Andre went outside for fresh air and waited for Clarence and Lesley. Surely Clarence would have no interest in this creepy place. After fifteen minutes he grew impatient and went back inside to speed things up. "Let's get moving," Andre said and went upstairs to find them. At the upstairs landing he walked toward the first bedroom on the right. Its door was open.

Lesley's underwear was on the floor. Her dress was pulled up and she was backed against the wall. Her legs were wrapped tight around Clarence's waist. "I have never done this before. I have never done this before! I love my husband!" she repeated over and over in breathless whispers while enjoying Clarence. Her fingernails jammed into his bare back.

They saw multiple homes fitting within Clarence's price range. Andre noticed most had well-stocked liquor cabinets, unusual in a dry county, he thought. "Rum, brandy, sherry—that's all for cooking," Lesley said.

"What about the vodka?" Andre asked sarcastically.

Poplar Grove had many old and beautiful religious buildings. They saw three large Baptist churches. Pearl River Bible Baptist was larger than a modern sports arena. Methodist, Lutheran, and Presbyterian chapels were located close together near Main Street. Clarence asked about Catholic churches. Lesley looked surprised. "There is a small area south of town across the train tracks. A few Catholics live back there. Locals call it the Catholic Ghetto. A priest drives up from Picayune every Saturday afternoon. They have mass in a rented strip mall. There are no real Catholic churches around here," she said.

The antebellum home on Michigan Avenue seemed perfect. Andre wondered why an old southern town would have a street named "Michigan" Avenue. Why did Louisiana have a Grant, Union, and Lincoln Parish? No one knew.

The house was in good shape and appeared to have always been well maintained. It had a new swimming pool in the backyard and a slave quarters at the property's far end. The front yard faced a ten-acre blueberry farm; the back faced the town's elementary school. Train tracks ran nearby at the bottom of the hill. The home was built in 1853 and had remained with the same family until now. Family members could not agree, and the home was being sold to settle the estate. "It reminds me of New Orleans," Clarence said. Andre was fascinated with the old slave quarters.

It was a dilapidated structure about fifteen by fifteen feet with a small covered porch, wooden walls, floor, and ceiling. At one time there had been a wood-burning stove in the center with a vent pipe extending through the roof. It had only one door and window. It had survived because kudzu vines covered it like a protective cocoon. A straw hat still hung on a nail inside to the right of the door. It could have been there for ten years or one hundred years. Andre loved the history of this place. Clarence seemed more interested in Lesley. They were back in the house screwing again.

The closing was a simple, stress-free affair since Lesley knew everyone at the courthouse and the lawyer was her cousin. Clarence rented a U-Haul truck, and they had everything moved in one weekend. On Sunday night Andre drove back to New Orleans, stopping at the Poplar Grove Shell station. He noticed an old van with Pennsylvania plates. A young black man was heading home and ran short of money after an unexpected repair bill. "Transmission rebuild was six hundred bucks!" he explained.

Andre gave him the hundred dollars cash he had in his wallet, shook his hand, and wished him luck. "Hope this helps." But the frightened station clerk called the sheriff and said a suspicious black man was harassing her customers. Two Pearl River County Sheriff cars arrived; one pulled in front, the other in the rear, boxing the van in. The deputies opened the van doors and began going through everything. The black man protested, explaining that he had rights. An officer turned in his direction. "Shut up, boy. You in Mississippi now!"

4

AS WITH ANY HOME PURCHASE, Clarence faced a number of unexpected surprises and expenses. A turtle managed to get into the pool. He swam around and around, trying to claw his way out, shredding the vinyl liner in the process. It was a 2,800-dollar expense to replace it. Clarence scooped the turtle out with a net used for removing leaves. He carried the turtle to the back of the property behind the slave quarters and gently placed it in the woods. "Be careful, lil fella," he said, setting the turtle free.

Clarence also asked Andre about mice removal. Andre suggested sticky pads. Most old homes in New Orleans had mice, and the sticky pads seemed to work better than traps. Clarence noticed that most droppings seemed to be in the central hallway. He placed multiple pads all around the hall and headed to work in New Orleans. "That should take care of the problem," Andre assured him confidently. Clarence arrived home late that evening and turned on the lights.

Old homes always have openings and unsealed areas that rodents find. Once inside they attract other unpleasant things. An old country home that has also been vacant is likely to have more of these issues. Clarence ran out of the house. He called Andre from his car, out of breath and scared. He locked the car doors and rolled up the car windows. "Andre, it's a snake! A snake in the house! A big damn snake!" The snake was at least six feet long and fatter than a "baseball bat," he said. It was a tangled mess, wrapped up with the sticky pads.

The Critter Getters said snakes were a common problem in the area because they are attracted to blueberry bushes and often find their way into homes. "Your neighbor's chicken coop certainly doesn't help either. But not to worry, most of these snakes are not poisonous," they said. After sealing some openings under the house they assured Clarence that everything was fine for now and they suggested he get a cat. Clarence had some sleepless nights ahead, but he did get two cats from the local "Stray Love" animal shelter. He named them Boudreaux and Trosclair.

Clarence's first monthly water bill was over four hundred dollars. That was in addition to the expense of refilling the pool. Andre thought he was mistaken. "That is impossible. Perhaps you're including the one-time hookup fee with the regular usage charge." Clarence said he knew how to read a water bill. Much of the Poplar Grove sewer pipes and treatment equipment was obsolete, and some of the system was nearly a century old. The Federal Environmental Protection Agency required a city-wide modernization. The Poplar Grove mayor and city council decided to pay for the new system over time from operating income.

They had no understanding of municipal bond markets, or perhaps they were reluctant to open city books and finances to municipal bond underwriters. Thus every property in town was assessed 350 dollars each month in addition to regular use charges. Clarence wondered how Lesley could forget to mention this. The city dumped the old water meters in a pile alongside a municipal building. Clarence looked through the discarded rubbish. He picked out two of the best meters, brought them home, and polished the brass by hand. He placed one on his bookshelf and gave the other to Andre.

Clarence was cutting his grass with a push mower. Each time he reached a certain area between the back of the house and the slave quarters, he noticed that the ground vibrated. He marked the spot with a twig, finished mowing, and returned with a shovel. Under a few inches of dirt he found a rusty piece of sheet metal. It covered a long-abandoned brick-lined well. Much of it had collapsed, but about fifteen feet remained. He called Andre. "Do you think there could be silver coins hidden there? Lesley said everyone hid their gold and silver from the Yankees," he explained. Clarence spent the weekend digging. He found a few broken dinner plates but no treasure. He replaced the sheet metal.

All of the interior walls were updated with sheetrock. Clarence wanted to hang pictures but did not want to make any unnecessary holes in his new walls. He carefully measured sixteen-inch intervals from the corners and tapped with his knuckles trying to find studs. Each picture hook hit solid wood on the first try. Clarence could not believe his luck. He soon realized that the sheetrock was covering original tongue-and-groove walls and ceilings. They removed the sheetrock in the living room, exposing the beautiful heart pine.

Clarence thought hosting a backyard barbeque would be a nice way to get to know his new neighbors. He invited Lesley and Spencer, her husband. "No, Clarence, I will not attend a backyard cookout. But I would love to attend a lawn party," Lesley said in a good-natured way. She said Clarence was like an old home: beautiful, strong, and useful but perhaps a little unrefined. He asked Andre, "What is a lawn party?" Andre told him lawn parties and barbeques were fundamentally the same, just with different names. Junior League members would never attend a cookout, but they loved lawn parties.

"Just tell her it's a lawn party and everything will be fine," Andre assured him.

Clarence invited Mr. and Mrs. Graves, the next-door neighbors, who raised chickens. George Graves weighed over three hundred pounds and was always dressed in the same dark blue overalls. His skin looked like it had never seen sunlight. It was white-pink and pasty like the glue used by elementary schoolchildren. He made a living working for the school board, where he oversaw bus maintenance. Mrs. Graves stayed home.

The doorbell was only a hole in the wall with two wires protruding out, and the button was missing. Clarence knocked. George opened his front door and studied Clarence for a long time. "What the fuck is a lawn party?" he finally asked and wondered aloud if Clarence associated with homosexuals in New Orleans. "Are you gay?" Things were cleared up once George understood that he was invited to a cookout. Mrs. Graves offered to bring sausage balls.

Clarence noticed a small glass jar on a living room shelf. "Is that a human tooth in that jar?"

Mrs. Adele Robins, Mr. Richmond Gains, and Mr. Isaac Groom were all invited personally by Clarence. Mrs. Bettie Whitfield suggested that Clarence cut down his magnolias. "They are the messiest trees. You will rake leaves year round," she said. Clarence loved old trees, especially hardwoods like magnolias. Mrs. Whitfield had been a widow since her husband died from an infected mosquito bite. She kept an artificial Christmas tree decorated year round. It was mounted on wheels and moved in and out of a living room closet each year as the holidays approached. Mrs. Robins promised to bring sweets prepared by the Methodist ladies. "Left over from our prison outreach," she explained. Mr. Gains told Clarence that he had been a friend of Charles Lindbergh, and Mr. Groom said he would love to attend. Everyone was coming and bringing friends.

Clarence prepared ribs, hamburgers, and chicken. As a special treat for his new Mississippi friends, he also prepared Creole Red Beans. People from New Orleans always used the camellia brand of red beans. They cooked up softer and creamier than all others. Clarence soaked the beans in water overnight. He was careful to pick over for stones. Looking for small stones in the beans was a New Orleans tradition from the days before modern processing and packaging techniques. Even today red bean packaging still suggests, "Pick Over for Stones."

In the morning Clarence drained the beans and drank the water that had absorbed the intense red bean flavor. "Bean liquor," Creoles called it. Add some vodka and a celery stalk, and it made a Creole Bloody Mary. Clarence added Andouille sausage and rice with the beans. Even in a wonderful plate of Creole Red Beans and Andouille sausage, you still needed to look out for stones. It was like life—just when things were going great, you bit down on a stone and cracked a tooth.

Clarence served soft drinks in Mason jars. Lesley brought wine and beer. Clarence asked about the liquor laws. "My husband is mayor," she reminded him with a friendly pat on his chin. Lesley's husband, Spencer, liked Clarence from the start and offered him a sales job at the Ford dealership. He was much older than Lesley and wore dress pants, a button-down collared white short-sleeve oxford shirt, and polished shoes. "Mayor is my part-time gig. My real job is running the dealership. I understand you're quite the salesman. Lesley says you can charm the pants off anyone." Spencer laughed and put his arm on Clarence's shoulder.

Clarence thought he looked like Thurston Howell III, the silly millionaire character on *Gilligan's Island*, with the exception of the strange "335" tattoo on his right arm. In New Orleans some people had a 504 tattoo—the phone exchange for the city. But 335 was not the Poplar Grove exchange.

I don't know what Lesley saw in him. Except that he kept her safe and warm.

Spencer asked Clarence about growing up in New Orleans. "Great town, but there sure are a lot of blacks there," he said and could not wait to tell a funny New Orleans story. Spencer said he brought his six-year-old neighbor and her family to New Orleans for the "Golden Key" ceremony. "The family employed a black maid," he explained. "When we arrived on Canal Street, my young neighbor looked around at all the blacks and asked her father, 'Why are there so many maids around here?'" Spencer laughed out loud and slapped Clarence's back. "She thought all blacks work as maids." He felt he had to explain the punch line because Clarence was not laughing. "Get it? All these maids!" Spencer repeated.

Clarence did sell cars for a time after high school. He did quite well but quit after his pay was cut. The owner felt he was making too much money. Clarence said he would consider Spencer's offer because the New Orleans commute was getting expensive. Really he wanted to be near Lesley. Spencer's jolly, happy-go-lucky demeanor seemed too rehearsed. His friendly veneer deliberately designed to disguise a sinister purpose. Despite his disarming doofus appearance, Andre was not fooled. He asked Clarence to be careful. "Don't underestimate him. I think he could be a dangerous adversary." Eventually even Shakespeare's Hamlet came to realize, "one may smile and smile and be a villain."

Lesley and Clarence had that secret lovers look when they were near each other. They stood too close, their hands brushed together often, and Lesley blushed. Andre hoped no one else noticed the obvious. Trying to distract Spencer's attention, he struck up a conversation about the new Fords. The lovers took the opportunity to sneak away like high school kids.

Clarence never worried about getting caught because he only pursued women who appeared to be happily married. He believed that when a marriage was on the rocks, the spouse would be on the lookout for unusual behavior. In a happy marriage the spouse had no reason to be suspicious. "Husbands won't notice the obvious because they see only what they want to see," he said. Mark Twain believed that once you had a reputation as an early riser, you could sleep till noon. Likewise, a reputation for faithfulness gave a woman a free pass to screw around. It was hard to argue with the logic of it all.

Clarence had successfully pulled sexual capers like this before. Clarence and Andre were on a road trip once and stopped at a roadside motel. It had a bar with a live band and a large local crowd. They struck up a conversation with a friendly couple sitting at the bar. Clarence eventually asked the wife to dance. He took her hand and led her to the crowded dance floor. Andre bought the husband another beer. Clarence and the woman left out a side door and went to the hotel room. They returned twenty minutes later. The husband was never any wiser.

The next-door neighbor, George Graves, was enjoying the party, but he constantly had his hand in his pants scratching his testicles. He said he fell asleep on his front porch while eating a jelly donut for lunch. It fell in his lap. He was wearing only boxer shorts and a T-shirt. Red ants were attracted to the sugar. They came and "bit my nuts real bad. They swelled up like baseballs." George explained to everyone that pouring aftershave "all over his nuts" only made the situation worse.

George enjoyed the chicken and hamburgers and ate many. He also liked beer. Clarence suggested a few drops of Tabasco on the hamburger for added creole flavor. George said he would not use Tabasco because he did not want "to get the cancer." George did not know the difference between Tabasco and tobacco.

"Those burgers were good. Where they from?" he asked.

Clarence said he bought the ground meat from the small butcher shop off Main Street. "It's to the right before you get to the train tracks. Next to the NAPA store."

George explained that no one bought meat there. "It's cheap because it is Negro meat. Only Negros shop there!" George was angry.

In his good-natured way Clarence planned to have a little fun at the expense of his racist neighbor. Late at night he walked past the slave quarters, through the kudzu, and into George Graves's backyard. Clarence repeatedly sneaked into George's henhouse and removed a few eggs. Then he strategically positioned the eggs inside the rooster cages. After a few weeks of this, George was convinced that somehow his roosters laid eggs. He went around town telling everyone the remarkable news. Then he went to the Agriculture Department of the community college for a meeting with the poultry research group. They politely suggested further research.

5

CLARENCE INITIALLY ENJOYED HIS NEW job at Spencer's Ford dealership. It was the only place to buy a new car in the area. If you wanted a Chevy or Buick, you had to drive to Hattiesburg or Gulfport to buy it. "Who wants to drive all over creation for routine warranty maintenance?" Clarence asked prospective buyers. He also reminded them that lax maintenance could void warranties. Most locals decided to go with the local convenience of Ford. After two months he was a top salesman. Without spending two hours commuting to New Orleans, Clarence had plenty of time to relax around his pool in the afternoon. He enjoyed the long summer days and arranged his work schedule with some evenings off. Boudreaux and Trosclair were always waiting on the front porch for him.

Locals enjoyed doing business with a dealership owned by the mayor. Some buyers even took pictures with Spencer. The mayor would never cheat them, many believed. When Clarence wasn't selling he liked to hang around in the service department. A black farmer came in with an old model pickup truck needing four "new" used tires.

"God forbid that I should drive any longer on them old tires," he said.

The service manager quoted a price of thirty-five dollars each. The farmer paid with small bills held in a worn-out brown wallet. The truck was placed on a lift and tires removed from the rims. The old tires were rolled around back. They were cleaned and mounted back on the rims. The poor farmer paid 140 dollars and left with the same tires he came in with. At least he was proud of his signed photo from Spencer, "With best wishes, the Mayor."

A young mother arrived with an overheated engine. She had three barefoot children in the backseat. Her unemployed husband recently left to find work in Texas, and she was having trouble managing everything alone. Clarence noticed a small leak in a hose. It could easily be cut shorter and reattached, solving the problem at no cost. But the service manager placed Alka-Seltzer tablets in the radiator.

With foam leaking everywhere he explained the "urgent need for a cooling system rebuild. An expensive job that will take some time," he said.

The young mother placed her head in her hands and cried. Clarence wondered why customers were treated with such contempt. "It's the dumb white crackers and poor blacks driving shitty cars that keep us in business," the service manager explained in a cavalier way.

Clarence had a small office near the side of the showroom. The showroom was large enough to hold four new cars. Some floor space was taken up by a restored 1951 Ford 8N farm tractor. The old tractor did attract people into the showroom. But they came to see how it was put together since they were still operating similar old tractors that were in constant need of repair.

The dealership's finance man, Mr. Robert, was called the "Special Man" because he was a problem solver, always able to arrange "special" financing for poorly qualified buyers. Robert and Spencer were old friends, but seemed complete opposites. Robert liked to wear dress slacks and brown leather shoes with white shirts; he kept three different sport coats hanging in the office and changed them throughout the day. He drove only Lincoln Continentals with blacked-out windows. Robert sat in an office across from Clarence near the stairs. A receptionist sat near the front door, and Spencer's office was upstairs. Spencer's office was decorated with jerseys and football helmets from Pearl River College teams. In 1982 the Wild-cats won a state title.

Clarence and Andre went to one home football game. A chain-link fence ran down the center of the home stands from the press box to the playing field. "A relic from the segregation era," according to Spencer. Blacks stayed on one side of the fence, whites on the other. "We don't encourage segregation anymore. They like to sit there, and we like to sit here. Simple as that," Spencer explained.

The game was an important social event for Poplar Grove. Some women wore their best starched dresses with heels, pearl necklaces, and bows in their hair. It looked like a convention of June Cleavers. The heels forced them to take tiny steps, waddling around the stands like penguins. "Andre, I wonder how the beaver is doing," Clarence asked as the wife of a pharmacist passed by, referring to the old TV show *Leave It to Beaver*.

She stopped in front of them and leaned over the railing, getting a better look at the action on the field. An unexpected breeze lifted her dress in the back. Unaware, she continued to lean forward, cheering the team. "Go Wildcats! Go Wildcats!" Her husband ran down the stairs and lowered her dress. She had a nice, attractive ass with tight, high-cut red underwear and a tattoo on her left cheek with the numbers 335. "Go Wildcats!"

Spencer's receptionist, Melissa, was twenty years old and had worked at the dealership for four years. "While in high school I enrolled in a 2+2 program that allowed students to work full time and finish with a diploma in four years," she explained to Clarence. He loved her silky southern accent and sexy young body. He said she had a nice "wiggle"! Melissa started working for Spencer when she was six-teen and had never held any other job.

"At eighteen I married my high school sweetheart. He also works for Spencer, as an oil change specialist."

Her husband never finished high school and had been in and out of the Pearl River County jail multiple times. The drug rehab programs had had only modest success. Melissa said she also handled bookkeeping and sales paperwork in addition to receptionist duties. It was not unusual for her to spend time in Spencer's office.

Occasionally Melissa's husband wandered into the showroom area to say hello. They would spend a few moments together, and then return to work. Quite often Melissa was not around. He would ask Mr. Robert, "Where is she?"

Clarence noticed that Robert reached under his desk and pushed a hidden button. The buzzer in Spencer's office warned that the husband was coming up the stairs. It was enough time for Melissa to pull up her underwear, straighten her skirt, and greet her naïve husband with an affectionate kiss on the cheek. Robert looked in Clarence's direction and realized that he knew what was going on.

"It's good to be king, and Spencer is king of Poplar Grove."

Melissa begged Clarence not to say anything. "My husband will get very angry, make a scene, and get fired. Where else can he find another job?" she asked. "He is a dropout junkie with a criminal record." Melissa said Spencer would most likely fire them both. "We need our jobs!" she said and reached over to unzip Clarence's pants. "I'll do anything you want," she begged.

Of course Clarence wanted Melissa, but he enjoyed sex on equal terms. He especially liked pursuing wealthy, upper-class partners. Those perceived to be way out of his league, the type of Junior League socialite who could never imagine screwing a Creole like Clarence until she was actually doing it and loving it. He would never take advantage of anyone's despair. It was not his style. Clarence moved her hand away, zipped up his pants, and assured Melissa her secret was safe.

"No charge," he said with his friendly smile.

That evening George Graves was waiting for Clarence in his front yard. "You trying to make a fool out of me?" he said angrily. He poked his finger at Clarence's chest. George explained that he found footprints leading from the kudzu to his chicken pens.

"Ain't no fucking roosters laying eggs!"

6

BOUDREAUX AND TROSCLAIR WERE NOWHERE to be found. Clarence looked around the house, even in the slave quarters. He called out, "Boudreaux, Trosclair. Boudreaux, Trosclair!" As he walked back toward the porch, Clarence heard weak sounds from under the steps. Boudreaux and Trosclair were lying side by side and appeared to be very sick. The veterinary office opened late after Clarence described the situation.

It took only a few moments for the vet to figure out what was wrong. "Do you work on cars at home?" he asked Clarence. The doctor explained that the cats had ingested antifreeze. "Animals are attracted to its taste and color," he said. "Antifreeze turns their kidneys to stone, resulting in a slow and very painful death. This could be an unfortunate accident, but it is also the preferred way ignorant people around here take care of unwanted animals. There is nothing we can do," he added.

After accepting the fact that Boudreaux and Trosclair faced a painful, drawn-out death, Clarence agreed to euthanize them. He held them both tight to his chest. He rubbed their ears between his thumbs and index fingers, an activity they both loved. He cuddled their faces next to his. Boudreaux purred.

Clarence was a lover but also a powerful fighter, especially when he was pushed too far. Once angered, his temper was fierce. He wanted to kill George Graves. Andre drove to Poplar Grove that night to calm things down.

"You need to be very smart about this because you will never prove that George did it deliberately," Andre explained to Clarence.

"He will expect a physical confrontation. He will be prepared for that. George may even try to instigate trouble. You need to stay calm and hit him from an unexpected angle." He told Clarence to avoid George's strengths but exploit his weaknesses.

"What does he love most?" Andre asked.

The next morning George was in his front yard trying to instigate a fight as expected. "How are your pussies doing? Haven't seen the little bastards in a few days," he yelled.

"Good morning, George." Clarence waved and headed to work.

The 1976 Chevy El Camino was George's pride and joy. It was half car and half pickup truck. He did the restoration himself, working on it during evening hours and on weekends. Much of the mechanical work was done at the school bus repair barn. The entire project took nearly three years to complete and many thousands of dollars. George was especially proud of the tractor-trailer chrome exhaust pipes he fabricated from a wrecked eighteen-wheeler. They extended through the pickup bed behind the back window. The truck was dark blue with flames painted on the hood. George spent most Saturday afternoons polishing the chrome wheels and exhaust pipes.

Clarence secretly snapped a few pictures and created ads on multiple Internet used car sites. George knew nothing about technology. "Must sell. Great condition. Fully restored. $600 cash or best offer." He placed the ads with George's home phone number and address. Clarence figured every hillbilly in Mississippi would show up to buy George's hotrod El Camino.

Soon, a large handmade sign affixed to a stick next to George's driveway illustrated his apparent frustration: "Fuck off, car not for sale. No theespassing." George must have skipped that part of second grade when spelling was taught.

"The FBI was here for ten years and never found out who lynched that Negro rapist, Mack Parker. You think you will ever find out who fed antifreeze to your cats? Good luck," George told Clarence.

"I never mentioned anything about antifreeze. How did you know about antifreeze? Who is Mack Parker?" Clarence asked.

Late that night George's wife called the sheriff to report him missing. "He left hours ago to feed the chickens and never returned." It was the deputy who heard George begging for help.

"I can't move. Help me. Please!" He cried like a baby.

Earlier that evening George had planned to sneak into Clarence's backyard. He intended to retrieve the bowl of antifreeze he had concealed near the back porch. The old piece of rusted sheet metal covering the brick well was strong enough to support Clarence's 180 pounds. George weighed over three hundred. It took a tow truck rigged with a special harness to lift him free. George claimed he was on Clarence's property looking for a runaway chicken when he fell into Clarence's "booby-trap."

7

LESLEY EXPLAINED HOW TO DO historic "research" at the local paper. She called the editor and asked him to assist Clarence with his interest. She incorrectly assumed he wanted to research the history of his house and the town. He did want to learn more about Poplar Grove, but he was also drawn to the name Mack Parker. "Remember, the *Gazette* is a small-town weekly newspaper. Nothing is on computer or even microfiche for that matter," she warned and described the damp basement where original issues of the paper were stored haphazardly in boxes.

"I think copies of nearly every Poplar Grove paper printed over the last one hundred and fifty years are in that basement." Lesley said it was an interesting place but poorly organized.

The editor explained his "filing" system and pointed out the boxes covering the Civil War, WWI, and the Great Depression. The room was large, with boxes stacked three high and two rows deep. Each individual box contained two years of papers. In the middle of the room was an oak table with five wooden chairs. The chairs had worn leather backs. The only two things on the table were an old glass ashtray and a reading lamp.

Clarence was surprised that smoking would be allowed in a room stacked floor to ceiling with old newspapers. He saw no fire extinguishers. A single hundred-watt light bulb extended from a wire in the ceiling centered over the table. The editor said smoking was not allowed, but no one ever bothered to remove the ashtray. He picked it up. "Sorry, but this is not the *Times-Picayune*." The editor was irritated.

"Civil War history is fascinating. However, I'm interested in a specific individual's name as well," Clarence said politely. "Mack Parker. Who is he? I have heard that name around town many times."

The editor's demeanor grew more agitated. He stopped cold in his tracks and stared at Clarence. He lowered his eyeglasses, tilted his head down, and looked at Clarence over the tops of his bifocals. "Nothing good happened here in 1959," he said and led Clarence back toward the WWI boxes. "Did you know that three Poplar Grove residents were on ships sunk by German U-boats? Very interesting," he insisted. The editor was annoyed by Clarence's persistence. "Look, son, you should never dig up the dead. Some things are better left buried. Leave it alone."

He nervously went back upstairs after pointing in the general direction of the more recent boxes. "I need to get back to work."

Clarence had to move some boxes to reach the one he was looking for. The search took time. He noticed that the 1959–1960 box was much lighter than the others. It seemed half empty. He brought it to the table.

"What are you doing?" Lesley asked from the top of the stairs.

Clarence assumed the editor had called her. She walked toward him with a sense of urgency. "Put that box back! Please!" It was more of a plea than a demand. "You have no idea what you're getting into." Clarence turned to face her. The bright light from the top of the stairs shone through her thin cotton dress, outlining her attractive figure. Clarence placed his hand under the dress, caressing her inner thigh. "This is dangerous. You have to stop!" she said, referring to Clarence's curiosity about Mack Parker, not their risky sex. Lesley was no longer worried about the dangers of their affair. She enjoyed it way too much for that.

She was fixing her hair and straightening her clothes. "Most likely you won't find much in that box anyway," Lesley said. "Go see your neighbor, Mr. Gains. You know, the gentleman who knew Charles Lindbergh. People say he's just a crazy old man. Don't let that fool you. You will be surprised how much Mr. Gains knows."

8

MR. GAINS WAS EAGER TO talk. He said it was true he knew Charles Lindbergh. Pan American World Airways hired Lindbergh as a consultant while Mr. Gains was a pilot. In the late 1950s Mr. Gains said he flew Boeing 707s from St. Louis to Mexico City, Buenos Aires, and Rio. On numerous trips Charles Lindbergh sat in the cockpit. They became friends. Mr. Gains had five shoe boxes filled with photos, flight charts, and Pan Am advertisements, brochures, and letters from Lindbergh. The young pilot in the picture, standing with six youthful flight attendants in Mexico City, barely resembled the tired old man now sitting across from Clarence. Mr. Gains smiled as he named the attendants, pointing each one out in the photo.

"Jill had beautiful red hair. Mary was captain of her college swim team. Elizabeth was from a small town in the Midwest," he said as he remembered happy times.

In 1958, a Tulane University grad student flew to Mexico City. She was researching a thesis involving colonial architecture and Latin culture. She fell in love with the dashing blue-eyed Pan Am pilot in his perfectly tailored uniform and easy smile. They were married three months later in Rio. Mr. Gains could not bear to be away from his lovely bride. He resigned from Pan Am and moved to her hometown, Poplar Grove. He took a job with a local crop-dusting firm.

"You wonder if I regret that decision to leave Pan Am?" He answered his own question. "No, never. Not for a single second. I had a good life," he assured Clarence. "Time does heal wounds. But time doesn't ease the uncertainty of regretful decisions made long ago. Over the years you just get used to living with the consequences of it all. We call it fate or destiny; some just call it life," Mr. Gains added while shifting through the boxes.

"There is one thing I regret deeply. I was a foolish young man." He became sad. "We were married thirty-five wonderful years before the cancer came. My lovely wife enjoyed afternoon baths in her Victorian claw-foot tub with red wine and soft music playing in the background. Brazilian jazz was always her favorite. I remember white linen drapes swaying in the summer breeze from the open bathroom windows. She asked me to join her a thousand times. She never grew tired of asking or frustrated with my selfish refusals. Those many clever excuses have spiraled around inside my head like restless ripples from stones I tossed into some pond long ago. I would gladly give everything for just one more opportunity. This time I would say yes. A thousand times, yes."

Saying his life was trouble free was like saying the weather was fine except for the hurricane. Looking down, Mr. Gains broke eye contact and seemed to be lost. How was it possible that a once vibrant life could be reduced to the contents of a few small boxes? *Time is a vicious opponent*, Clarence thought. *It defeats all challengers unconditionally. Some, like Mr. Gains, keep a few old photos and letters to ease the pain of loss. In the end it makes no difference.*

A card, about the size of a driver's license, caught Clarence's eye. Printed on the left side was a black-and-white photo of a handsome young man in a business suit. "Vote for Jeff Gains, ALDERMAN" was printed in red, white, and blue ink.

"I was looking for excitement. Something to do other than crop dusting. So I ran for public office," he explained.

Mr. Gains won a four-year term as town alderman in November 1959. He ran at large and actually received more votes than the mayor did. "Your friend Lesley, her mother was my campaign manager. She organized one heck of a race. Yes, she did!" Mr. Gains was comfortable campaigning in the poor neighborhoods of Poplar Grove and had friends from Rio help organize the black voters. "It was something no white candidate had ever done. Really shook things up. Yes sir. Really shook this town up!

"The first thing the campaign did was purchase ten broken-down old lawnmowers and rakes," he said. Blacks found walking in white neighborhoods were usually questioned by the police and arrested. "But blacks could go anywhere without trouble if they were pushing lawnmowers. Our black campaign workers were able to get around town without incident. They enjoyed the cat and mouse of it all," he explained. Clarence asked about Mack Parker.

"You need to remember this was before the Selma marches and Montgomery boycotts," Mr. Gains said. "I met Mack while campaigning door to door in his neighborhood. He became a very efficient political organizer and my friend. Soon he was in charge of organizing campaign volunteers and Election Day get-out-the-vote activities. He learned to love public speaking and gave many speeches around town. If things went wrong, I risked the embarrassment of losing an election, but Mack risked his life. He was no rapist! He loved his wife and family too much. Mack never looked for trouble. All he ever wanted was the right to participate in the political system without intimidation or threats."

On Election Day Mack monitored polling stations in the town's black wards as voting closed. Ballots were placed in slits cut into the tops of wooden boxes secured with a padlock. Only the election commissioner had a key. Late that evening a Ford pickup truck with suspicious young white men began circling the block. Four or five were riding in the truck's bed. Two were in the cab. They called the driver "Spence." His real nickname was Scalper, but no one was brave enough to call him that to his face.

"We hear you are disrupting the election, boy!" Spence said to Mack.

"They planned to stuff the ballot box," Mr. Gains explained.

Mack refused to leave. The men jumped from the back of the truck with baseball bats. They walked toward Mack, swinging the bats. Mack stood tall with his arms at his side. "If you are not disrupting the election, why are you here? Poplar Grove does not have race problems. You are the problem. We raced over to protect the ballots. You see no race problems here." Spence clubbed Mack in the ribs. They promised to return and teach Mack a "real lesson, real soon!"

"They came back all right. In 1959, a Mississippi black man accused of raping a white woman was as good as dead," Mr. Gains said. Because of the sexual nature of the charges, the female victim was never publicly identified. "Mack did not have the opportunity to face his accuser in a courtroom. There was never a broken-down car. The husband never walked away. The white woman was never alone on a deserted Mississippi highway, and a rape never occurred. Mack Parker was framed. The alleged victim was in fact a seventeen-year-old, troubled pregnant girl from Hattiesburg. Her boyfriend was also seventeen. She was paid two hundred dollars to make the fabricated rape charge and identify Mack," he said.

"But the newspapers did say Mack Parker was questioned by police and he was 'positively identified' by the alleged victim," Clarence questioned.

"Mack was the only black man in the police lineup, and they interrogated him for sixteen straight hours. They beat that written confession out of him," Mr. Gains said. "Medical examiners reported the rape victim was 'impregnated with black seed,' causing an explosion of anger in the white community. They wanted Mack out of politics and out of Poplar Grove forever.

"Things got out of control quickly, and that hatred resulted directly in Mack's lynching at the hands of a hooded mob. Mack was innocent. I know because the woman gave birth to a white child in a Biloxi hospital. I discovered her name in discarded court records found in the 1990s. At that time a newly elected county clerk promised to computerize court records. Most old paper files were carelessly thrown out with the trash. The 'Mack' files were moved multiple times. That explains why they were lost for over thirty years, until I found a small group of records in the trash," Mr. Gains said.

Clarence asked about Mack's family.

"They were turned into paupers overnight. His family lost their home, their bank account, and their dignity. Mack had placed a small plot of ground in his wife's name. That was the only asset not seized by the authorities. Unable to cope, Mack's wife separated the children between different family and friends spread across southern Mississippi. She was left without employment or prospects. She died a few years later in a state facility for the insane. Mack's son has grown up believing his father was a rapist. He's been in and out of trouble for years. It's all very sad," Mr. Gains said.

"What was the pregnant girl's name?" Clarence asked.

"Her name was Graves. She died a few years ago. But her son still lives in Poplar Grove. His name is George. George Graves. Your next-door neighbor!" Mr. Gains said to a surprised Clarence. "In the end only one thing really matters. The dead should count on resting peacefully. Everyone deserves a comfortable grave.

Mr. Gains explained that in the Hindu religion, people are reincarnated over and over, either paying for past sins or being rewarded for living a virtuous life in some previous existence. "No one rests peacefully until perfection is achieved. But the DNA from all those past lives contributes to our individuality. We are prisoners of our past experience. We can't escape that reality. How is it possible to overcome so many mistakes in only one lifetime? It's not. That is why hatred keeps going on and on, forever. There is no peace for the living. There is no peace for the dead. Every grave is uncomfortable," Mr. Gains reasoned.

9

"**MACK BELIEVED THE DEFINITION OF** a man includes the right to make important decisions. Many of these decisions take place in a voting booth." Mr. Gains had a question for Clarence. "You asked if I harbored any regrets. I was out of town on that terrible day. For all these years I have been unable to clear my friend's name. Can you help?"

"Lesley cares for you very much. The fact that you are Creole does not bother her. She is beautiful, smart, and very strong willed, just like her mother." Mr. Gains handed Clarence a stack of old folders. "I have been swimming against the currents of this sad little town for decades. I'm tired," he said, and the two men shook hands good-bye.

Andre was happy to look over the folders and documents but warned Clarence that decades had passed. It was most unlikely that evidence of the murder or witnesses willing to testify remained. "Besides, the FBI has reopened many of the old desegregation-era hate crime investigations. If there was anything new, they would certainly have found it. The US Department of Justice has unlimited resources." Not discouraged, Clarence said they could meet with Mr. Gains anytime.

"Andre, you know people change. Maybe now someone will be willing to talk to you. You are much smarter than the FBI," Clarence said with his usual smile.

"Okay, Clarence. We'll see what's going on."

Soon thereafter, Mr. Gains was placed in Saint Ann's nursing home by "concerned" family. His most treasured possessions were dumped haphazardly in boxes and placed on the curb with other useless trash. The Pan Am photos washed into a storm drain during an early fall shower. Enthusiastic family members kept everything they could easily sell: chairs, tables, and dishes.

They organized a garage sale the following week. All of Mr. Gains' remaining possessions were placed on the front lawn. Chairs were listed at twenty-five dollars each. Tables were listed at seventy-five dollars. His antique armoires sold for 125 dollars each. Smaller items were selling for a few bucks. A 150-year-old, seven-foot-tall grandfather clock was priced at three hundred dollars. It sold first. His wife's favorite claw-foot tub sold for thirty-five dollars.

Buyers began arriving early, many with pickup trucks or rented U-Hauls. By noon most everything was gone. The family ended the sale early, and the few remaining items were marked down to nothing or placed on the curb for the garbage truck to pick up. When the proceeds were divided, each family member received about nine hundred dollars. "Now that all this useless crap is gone, we can sell the house," the nephew said.

10

GREEK PHILOSOPHERS TAUGHT THAT IT is necessary to invest trust and great power in political leaders because only powerful rulers can protect us from social corruption and disorder. But what happens when our leaders themselves resort to corruption and plunder? Most criminals and crimes are local, trivial matters; how much more damage can someone with criminal intent do when they wield the power of government?

Clarence enjoyed having donuts and coffee at the same little Main Street shop early every Saturday morning. Andre could tell he was excited when he called. "The governor is here! The governor," he said. Andre told him that most likely he had a meeting or campaign event in town. "Not the Mississippi governor. The Louisiana governor! He's here in Poplar Grove!" Clarence was thrilled to meet him.

No longer interested in owning timber land, the Bogalusa paper company began selling off many thousands of acres in the Poplar Grove area. The American paper mill industry faced difficult times. Foreign competition from modern mills made older, inefficient American mills economically obsolete. The Bogalusa company desperately sold off most assets to strengthen a dying balance sheet.

The sudden availability of so much inexpensive land caused a dramatic and fast drop in prices overall. In many areas the cost of an acre fell to less than four hundred dollars. Louisiana politicians and businessmen began buying large parcels, taking advantage of this "once in a lifetime" opportunity. Poplar Grove was close enough to Louisiana yet far outside the reach of many annoying Pelican State laws. It was the perfect place to plan misadventure, skullduggery, and play.

Louisiana Sunshine Laws made it a crime for three or more elected officials to meet in secret for the purpose of discussing official state business. However, it was not illegal to get together and hunt quail or fish in Mississippi. Poplar Grove was outside the reach of reporters from the *Picayune* and *Morning Advocate*, Louisiana laws, and suspicious spouses. "You newspaper boys have no jurisdiction here on my Poplar Grove property," the Louisiana governor said as he closed the gate to his private drive.

The Louisiana attorney general, governor, insurance commissioner, Secretary of State, and two state senators purchased Poplar Grove property. The owner of Louisiana's largest grocery store chain, the governor's friends, and some state contractors and vendors eventually owned land here. One state senator rented his 800-square-foot, three-room Poplar Grove cabin to a Baton Rouge lobbyist for $30,000 per week. Kickbacks were never proven, but the fair market value for the rental was about $300 per month. Politicians often used this rental tactic to collect bribes. The illegal funds could be reported to the IRS as income, thus eliminating one possible source of legal trouble.

"You can find more Louisiana politicians hiding in Poplar Grove than working in Baton Rouge," complained the *Times-Picayune*.

The Louisiana governor bought a home, barn, and airstrip. An automatic iron gate secured the entrance, with a long driveway lined by azaleas and tall pines leading deep into his private acreage. The governor's initials were attached unevenly to the front gate. They were deliberately lopsided because people said the governor was crooked! Everyone wanted to get invited to one of the governor's infamous Poplar Grove parties.

Russell Burley was short and fat. His jaw was too small for his face, and his eyes were too close together, but he was very rich. His first profitable scam involved Craftsman Tools manufactured and sold by Sears. These wrenches and sockets were high quality, American made, and expensive.

Sears offered a no-questions-asked cash lifetime return policy. While visiting a New Orleans flea market, Russell happened upon a gentleman selling cheap knock-off Craftsman tools made in Taiwan. They looked exactly like authentic Craftsman products. Russell purchased the entire bogus inventory for a few hundred dollars cash money.

"Cash talks. Bullshit walks," the flea market salesman said.

Sears was the Wal-Mart of its day with stores in nearly every city. After six months Russell had returned the entire inventory of fake Craftsman tools for full cash refunds. Sears employees never asked a single question. Russell's net profit was fourteen thousand dollars.

Another of his companies, Systems for Learning, made a fortune selling educational software to Louisiana's sixty-six local school systems. His educational material was guaranteed to teach reading and writing to third graders. The governor granted Russell "sole source" vendor status. His contracts were not subject to a competitive bid process. A member of the state education board asked why they had to buy such expensive software.

"Because I am a friend of the governor. That's why!" Russell said.

Russell paid an old alcoholic remedial math teacher at the University of New Orleans three hundred dollars to record his class lectures. The DVDs were packaged into high school math tutoring workshops for students falling behind. The Louisiana legislature then required the program for every student assigned remedial math based on ACT scores. The math teacher eventually sued Russell for two million dollars. He claimed he was entitled to a percentage of the profits. His petition was dismissed without merit by an appointed state judge. The university fired him for the "inappropriate use of university property." He told the *Times-Picayune* he wished he never heard of Russell Burley and his stupid DVDs.

Russell was one of the secret twenty-five names on the governor's special friends list. Being on this list was lucrative. However, he was always expected to do whatever the governor wanted. He could be asked to fund an unknown local political candidate in a small parish, enter a political race himself, set up an opponent's wife, deliver a bribe, or pick one up. Russell could be a wheelman or a bagman. He was even expected to share his girlfriends. He could never say no to the governor.

He usually ate lunch at the same Baton Rouge steak house every day. He insisted on Syracuse china and Reed and Barton silverware. Russell was at least sixty-eight years old but loved to dine with young women. They were seduced by his wealth and power or interested in moving up in one of his companies. His young dining guests caressed his arm and looked on in admiration as he ate. He usually concentrated on the porterhouse, barely acknowledging their presence.

Russell owned a twin-engine private airplane. When not visiting his own property, he often flew to the governor's Poplar Grove estate for weekend parties. Each time, he brought a different woman. After determined persistence, a gorgeous secretary finally agreed to his suggestive invitation. She was tall, with red hair and large breasts, and she still had the body of the LSU track star she was ten years before.

The governor was waiting when Russell and his friend landed at his airstrip. A state limousine was parked nearby, a uniformed Louisiana state trooper at the wheel. Governor Edwards looked puzzled. "You with Russell?" he asked the redhead. "Usually he brings only Mexicans or Blacks." The governor put his arm around her. They walked off together, leaving Russell alone.

John owned Louisiana's largest chain of grocery stores. He won an election to the Louisiana Public Service Commission by promising to reduce the price of milk. "Your baby deserves affordable milk," he said over and over during the campaign. It made no difference to him that the commission had very little to do with the price of dairy products.

John's Poplar Grove acreage covered a large remote area. Local rednecks liked to sneak around and grow a few marijuana plants here and there. They lived on food stamps and in government-subsidized housing but could afford nice pickup trucks and automatic weapons. Drug Enforcement Agency helicopters routinely flew over these areas looking for the hidden marijuana fields. When the DEA discovered weed growing on a remote area of John's property, he blamed it on his "dumbass" foreman and "trespassing rednecks." The marijuana arrest was not his only problem; John was also in deep financial trouble.

He purchased a competing grocery chain of fifteen "super" stores. But the chain did not replenish their shelves. John bought empty stores. Because of mounting debt, he was unable to obtain short-term financing. He now owned fifteen empty new stores and was unable to restock his original stores as well. Employees from both chains went on strike when John proposed wage reductions. According to price surveys, John's milk was now the most expensive in a five-state area.

Russell Burley called his Poplar Grove property "The Foxhole." Once each year he held the famous "Representative Roundup." All Mississippi and Louisiana state senators and representatives were invited to attend a wild Poplar Grove weekend involving beer, barbeque, live bands, a dove hunt, and target shooting competitions. Hundreds attended, driving to Poplar Grove in their official state vehicles. The *Times-Picayune* claimed Russell was trying to buy influence. The elected officials were accused of using state vehicles for personal business.

Russell told the paper to "go to hell!"

Poplar Grove police arrested two *Times-Picayune* reporters snooping around the Roundup. They were charged with trespassing, resisting arrest, battery against a police officer, and threatening an elected official. Each reporter faced a potential fifteen-year prison sentence. They were held overnight in the overcrowded Pearl River County Jail. Fifteen other men were held in the same small cell. The reporters slept on cold cement near an open toilet. On Monday morning all charges were dropped and the two reporters were released.

"Next time I won't be so lenient. You boys be careful 'round here," the Mississippi judge advised. He then left the courthouse and met Spencer for breakfast.

The *Times-Picayune* claimed the reporters had been kidnapped by corrupt Mississippi police officers to protect "this secret Sodom and Gomorrah of political misadventure hiding in the pine forests of Poplar Grove." The reporters swore they would never set foot in Mississippi again.

"A corrupt shit hole," one reporter said off the record.

Spencer was invited to and participated in many of these parties and events. The Louisiana boys wanted to know and trust the mayor of Poplar Grove. The deeper involved Spencer became, the more they liked him. He was less likely to cause trouble if he was guilty of the same sins, they reasoned. They were especially pleased with his handling of the two *Times-Picayune* reporters. Spencer was invited to Russell's for afternoon drinks on his back deck. He brought Melissa along to meet his "important new friend." He asked her to be neighborly.

When they arrived Russell was already in his hot tub on the back deck. He had a Maker's Mark on the rocks in his left hand. An unlit cigar was in the other. He offered both Spencer and Melissa cigars and drinks. A gold chain was nearly hidden by his thick black chest hair.

"So this is your little country friend I have heard so much about," Russell said, referring to Melissa. "Nice to meet you, baaaaby. You sure look sweet."

Russell stood up and pulled down his bathing suit. He looked like a hairy hippo emerging from a river on some Nature Channel show. He motioned for Melissa.

"Mr. Russell is a very important man. Be nice," Spencer encouraged her.

Russell placed his hands behind her neck and forced her head downward. Melissa once thought Spencer liked her. Now there was no doubt how he really felt. "We need to introduce you to the governor. He will like you," Russell said when he was finished.

Politicians and sex scandals went hand and hand. Power was an aphrodisiac, and most politicians were perverted anyway. The prospect of easy sex had always been a motivating factor in the choice of political careers. Bill Clinton, Wilbur Mills, Gary Hart, Mel Reynolds, and even Alexander Hamilton had national sex scandals. Warren Harding had affairs with Carrie Phillips and Nan Britton while he was married and president. Power and sex went together. It was the same in Poplar Grove as it was in Washington, DC.

It was Russell who encouraged Spencer to donate his radioactive drilling pipe to the city of New Orleans. Once Tulane discovered the problem, Russell blamed city engineers for not doing their jobs. He landed a lucrative contract to do decontamination work.

Even the commission of a minor legal infraction became a federal issue once the conspirers crossed state lines. The FBI was not known for a sense of humor regarding political corruption, especially when it involved multiple states. Most politicians were careful to keep things close to home. Not these cavalier Louisiana and Mississippi knuckleheads.

11

ANDRE ASKED CLARENCE HOW SPENCER treated Lesley. "She never really talks about him much. I'm not sure. But I don't think Lesley would put up with anything like that. I really don't think he cares. The marriage has definitely hit the rocks," Clarence said. Andre suggested he begin keeping notes on everything he could learn about Spencer's business interests. "It may come in handy someday. Just make sure you don't get caught. Be very careful."

Clarence said Spencer had some type of deal with local insurance agencies. Each time a late model Ford, Lincoln, or Mercury was totaled in an accident, Spencer was called. His mechanics removed nearly every useable part, even the tires. These parts were cleaned, labeled, and stored in a warehouse behind the dealership. When Spencer's mechanics did warranty work, they never used factory new parts. They installed used parts from the secret warehouse but charged factory prices. Spencer's profit margin was nearly 100 percent when customers paid for new.

Clarence believed Spencer's people actually stole cars from their own customers. Each time an expensive Lincoln was sold, the dealership kept a set of keys. Shortly thereafter they returned to the customer's home and drove away with the car. It was stripped down and the rolling frame was left in an area where it would be found by the Poplar Grove Police Department.

The insurance companies sold the stripped vehicles as a total "theft loss." Spencer bought the frames with clear titles. He had the cars reassembled and sold them on his used car lot at full value. Insurance policies compensated the victims. Often they returned to buy another new car from Spencer.

A recent theft attempt nearly turned tragic. Two thieves waited around the corner in a Ford pickup truck with the engine running. The other thief walked past the target house, where a Lincoln was parked in the carport. The house seemed quiet. The night was dark. Spencer's hired thief confidently walked toward the Lincoln. Chihuahuas are small dogs, but they can make a lot of noise. Three of the small barking dogs were in a fenced area behind the Lincoln. A woman opened the kitchen door.

"Harry, get the shotgun! Some punk is trying to steal the Lincoln!" she yelled from behind a screen door.

"Come here, you little bastard!" Harry yelled as he fired off three twelve-gauge shots. He was overweight and out of shape. The young thief ran very fast.

"Let's go! Get out of here!" the thief yelled as he leaped over the tailgate and dove headfirst into the pickup's bed, keeping his head down. Harry managed one more shot aimed at the back of the truck as it sped away. He dropped the shotgun and placed his hands on his knees, trying to catch his breath.

"I'm too old for this shit! Bastards."

Andre was interested in Spencer's deal with the insurance agents. "What are they getting out of this?" It could be something as simple as money, although it was most likely much more complicated than that. Money by itself could not create the long-term loyalty commitments necessary to pull this off. Spencer offered something more enticing.

Probably something of a sexual nature, Andre thought.

It didn't stop there. Spencer realized that most people had absolutely no idea what type of tires were on their new cars. When cars came in for their first scheduled service, Spencer had the original tires removed. They were replaced with some from the wrecked cars. The dealership then had another set of "new" tires to sell to someone else. Spencer had the cars washed and tires cleaned and blackened with a shiny substance. The cleaning hid any obvious evidence that the tires were used.

The dealership offered $15.99 complete oil changes, "using the best oil available," according to ads running in local newspapers. The price went up once customers were convinced to purchase the "Engine Shampoo." The secret shampoo was nothing but a quart of mineral spirits in a special can that claimed to reduce carbon deposits and eradicate gunk buildup. It was added to the crankcase with the old oil. The engine was run for twenty minutes, then drained. The treatment cost an additional one hundred and twenty dollars. It did absolutely nothing to benefit the engine. Melissa's husband did most of the work in the "oil change department." He said the treatment could actually damage bearings and cranks inside the engine.

Spencer screwed everyone, not just the "uneducated blacks and poor whites." But unsuspecting customers were happy when their cars were returned washed, polished, and shampooed. "We love this deal-ership," one family said as they referred other family members. "They always treat us right!" Spencer said he went the extra mile because he realized the value of happy customers. The dealership had received multiple Chamber of Commerce awards for "Outstanding Service and Customer Satisfaction." The Poplar Grove Better Business Bureau chapter awarded Spencer their highest rating.

12

MR. GAINS' VICTORIAN HOME WAS listed for sale with a real-estate firm in Hattiesburg. Lesley said the family hired an out-of-town real-estate firm because she was unwilling to do it. "I refuse to sell his home. I won't do it," she said. She also asked Andre about the legality of a suspicious Power-of-Attorney document Mr. Gains signed. "His son placed a lot of papers in front of him. He had no idea what he was signing. He would never agree to sell his home," Lesley insisted.

The home was painted a pale yellow and was located on two acres adjacent to the train tracks. The property was full of mature oaks and magnolias. It was a two-story Victorian with a wraparound front porch with spirals on each side. Built by carpetbaggers in the 1870s, the home had retained most of its priceless architectural features, including the original staircase and marble mantels on each of its seven fireplaces. Original heart pine floors were intact throughout. The bedrooms were carpeted in one of the few concessions to modern comforts. Mr. Gains liked it that way. The address was 300 West Michigan Avenue, but most locals knew the home simply as "Disraeli."

Mr. Gains admired Benjamin Disraeli, the great British prime minister during the late 1800s. A brass plaque near the driveway read "Disraeli" in large letters; below, in much smaller print, was the actual street address. To the right of the front door was another plaque placed there by Mr. Gains.

What we anticipate seldom occurs.

But what we least expect generally happens.

Benjamin Disraeli

Mr. Gains currently resided in room 32A on the second floor of the Saint Ann's Home in a rundown area between Slidell and Bogalusa, Louisiana, on Highway 21. He had a single bed, one small dresser, a vinyl chair, and a magazine rack. All of the furniture looked like salvage from a cheap highway motel. The mattress was covered with a hard plastic protective liner. His room measured twelve by fourteen feet. On each side of the bed there was barely enough room to turn around. In a small picture frame on the dresser was a photo of a Boeing 707 cut out from a magazine. A dirty window looked out over a parking lot and the back of a rundown strip mall. Andre's Tulane dorm room was larger and better furnished.

The mall housed two tattoo shops, a sandwich shop, a Korean nail polish salon, a clothing consignment business, a bar, and the Okinawa Massage Parlor. Mr. Gains thought prostitutes might work at the massage business. Metal trash bins lined the road behind each business. Every Wednesday morning a garbage truck appeared and automatically raised the bins on metal arms, dumping the contents into the back of the truck. Mr. Gains sat and sat, waiting each week to watch the truck.

Mr. Gains had one friend at Saint Ann's. Richard Tower was too young to be in a nursing home. He was in his fifties. He'd never smoked, but his wife had for decades. Mr. Richard developed emphysema from the secondhand smoke and underwent prolonged treatment. Medical professionals said his wife would have to quit smoking immediately for her husband's sake.

"Only a cessation of smoking can stop the disease progression," the doctor warned.

Instead of quitting cigarettes, she committed Mr. Richard to Saint Ann's. "It's for his own good," she insisted. She still smoked three packs a day. Mr. Richard had not seen his wife or left Saint Ann's in five years.

The federal government will cover nursing home expenses only if all personal assets have been exhausted first. Many families have tried to hide wealth by transferring property or selling below market value to family. In New Orleans a wealthy grandmother secretly transferred jewelry to her granddaughters. The transaction was discovered once the government subpoenaed the family's insurance policies.

"The items were insured last year. Where are they now?" the government auditor asked. The government will aggressively "claw back" assets when Medicare fraud is suspected.

Trying to avoid these issues, Mr. Gains' family found the absolute cheapest nursing home available. By paying out of pocket, they were betting that he would die quickly before the cash ran short. The sooner he died, the more money they pocketed for themselves. With the potential sale of the house, the antique furniture sale, and liquidation of other assets, it could be quite lucrative for all involved. No family members had been to visit or even called Mr. Gains.

They arrived at Saint Ann's just before lunch. A sign near the road read, "A CARING PLACE FOR YOUR LOVED ONES." Lesley walked in first; Clarence and Andre followed close behind. The smell was overpowering. Bleach, pine oil, urine, feces, and ammonia created a stench that made their eyes water and stomachs turn. "I feel sick," Clarence said. Elderly people sat in a television room to the left. Some had soiled pants. They all stared in the direction of an old Zenith TV in a faux wooden cabinet. But it was off.

"Why don't you turn the television on?" Andre asked the woman behind the front desk.

"It's broke. That's why," she said while eating fried chicken from a lunch box. She did not look up.

Lesley asked why the residents were not clean. "I don't clean bottoms at lunch," the receptionist said, licking chicken grease off her fingers.

"Looks like they haven't had a bath in weeks!" Lesley demanded to see the head nurse.

"I am the head nurse," the woman said.

Andre advised Lesley to take it easy, reminding her that Mr. Gains lived here. "There are proper ways to handle this," he assured her.

"Is this dump even licensed?" Clarence asked Andre.

"Licensed for now," Andre said as he placed a call to his legal staff in New Orleans.

They found their way to the elevator. When the door opened on the second floor, Mr. Gains was waiting to greet them. He hugged Lesley and Clarence. They embraced for a long time. Clarence introduced Andre. Mr. Gains shook his hand. Andre suggested they all go out for lunch. Mr. Gains became very nervous.

"I don't think I'm allowed to just leave like that," he said.

"That will not be a problem," Andre said confidently. Clarence and Lesley invited Mr. Richard to join them. They all walked past the front desk. The "head nurse" jumped up. "Unauthorized outings are not allowed!" Andre handed her his card, "LEAD LITIGATOR - Jones, Adams and Dunbar." She mumbled something under her breath, sat down, and went back to her fried chicken.

Clarence and Lesley asked if Andre could do anything to help the residents of Saint Ann's. "Not to worry! I have already called my legal team. Inspectors and investigators from the Federal Department of Health and Human Services and Adult Protective Services will be at Saint Ann's at eight next Monday morning. Two lawyers from my firm will be with them as well." Andre explained that multiple legal avenues were being prepared and considered. "First we need to determine who actually owns Saint Ann's. Then we need to research all inspection reviews and records of complaints and code violations. Expect charges of felony criminal neglect and abuse and exploitation of the elderly," Andre said, eager to shut Saint Ann's down.

13

THIS SATURDAY MORNING, MARK, THE young assistant manager of the Poplar Grove Food Cougar, was running almost two hours late. His career started six years before, when he was a student at Pearl River County High School, delivering groceries on a bicycle after school. Now he worked eight consecutive ten-hour days, and the exhaustion was taking a heavy toll. Mark did not remember hearing the alarm clock ring or turning off the snooze button. Today he was scheduled to run the store on his own, but recently he'd had trouble balancing the cash accounts. Two experienced cashiers quit. They claimed he was "fanatic about stupid details." One cashier used the word "anal."

Saturday was always a busy day for grocery stores. But this was unusual. Finding a parking space in the small storefront lot was difficult. Some cars had Louisiana plates. Finally Mark parked his old Chevy on a side street around the corner. He loved cars, especially sports cars and convertibles. He studied their mechanical features and production histories. Mark dreamed of the day when he could afford a Jaguar or Maserati sports car.

The young manager ran to the store, clip-on necktie in hand, shoes untied. It was never necessary to lock his car. No one would steal the rusty junk. His official blue uniform shirt was unbuttoned. His name tag and assistant manager badge were left at home. This was his first real job since graduating top in his class from Pearl River College with an associate degree in business administration. He was accepted at Vanderbilt and Sewanee but was unable to afford the fees. Mark was eager to do well and disappointed in himself for running late.

"Managers must always set a good example for the other employees. Managers must always set a good example…" He repeated this line, memorized from his management training program. The manager's office was on a raised platform in front of the five cash registers. It provided clear views of the entire store. He enjoyed surveying his domain.

This was the swingers weekend. The host couple arrived at the Food Cougar promptly at 10 a.m. and began filling a shopping cart with various items like regular shoppers would do. He worked at the nearby Stennis Space Center, and she was a high school history teacher, the second daughter of a Methodist preacher. They had been married seven years and members of the swingers club for about five years. It was a faithful marriage, with the only exception being the monthly swinger parties. This was their first opportunity to serve as hosts.

Eventually they made their way over to the produce section and picked out a fresh pineapple. The woman raised her eyebrows in a flirtatious way. Her husband carefully placed the pineapple upside down in the cart. Russell stood nearby, trying to be inconspicuous. He had plenty of time to fly to Baton Rouge, pick up four senate interns, and return.

The two pushed the cart around the store twice. She looked at other shoppers, wondering if they were waiting for the upside-down pineapple signal. Most likely, she'd already had sex with most men in the store, but during swinger events everyone was required to wear masks. They selected Mardi Gras masks, monster masks, animal masks, historical figures, or opera masks. Some wore full costumes. All identities remained secret. Anticipating sex with fifteen to twenty masked strangers was extremely exciting. She loved variety. She especially enjoyed multiple lovers from various angles. Her husband enjoyed watching. Letting his wife screw so much was a good way to keep the marriage strong, he reasoned.

Her erect nipples caught his attention. When they reached a quiet back aisle, her husband reached his left hand under her dress. He was right-handed but always used his left for this. "Stop! We can't do this here!" she said while giggling, playfully slapping his hand away. He lifted her up and sat her on top of a display of Idaho potatoes. With his thumb he moved her underwear to the side, then penetrated her with three fingers. She unzipped her husband's pants.

The young couple enjoyed "dogging" almost as much as they liked swinging. Having sex in public view was always an erotic thrill. On Saturday evenings they often drove to New Orleans and found a place to park in a crowded area. The French Quarter worked well. They fooled around in the car's backseat with the windows down. She especially liked when voyeuristic strangers reached in the car and touched her.

The young manager worked fast to get himself squared away. Mark tied his shoes, buttoned his shirt, and clipped on his necktie. He combed his hair, then called the main office in Hattiesburg to explain his tardiness. His job was secure for now, but any more mistakes or commotion could be a problem for his young career. Mark stood with his hands on the platform railing and looked over the store, confident his day would get better.

Everything seemed to be in order. Long lines at the deli counter were a good sign. Cold cuts and lunch sandwiches were the store's most profitable items. Each checkout line was two or three shoppers deep. He sent a stock boy out to collect shopping carts from the parking lot. All departments were operating smoothly as expected. Then something very unusual caught his eye at the far end of the last aisle. He leaned forward to improve his line of sight.

"Who has sex in a grocery store? This is a family environment! For Christ's sake!"

He leaped down the platform stairs, covering two or three steps with each stride. Still disbelieving his own eyes, he turned left and ran toward the last aisle. Mark told a mom with two young children, "Stay right here. Don't go near the potatoes!" The swingers quickly slipped out a side exit, leaving no evidence or witnesses. The manager saw the taillights of their SUV heading south on Main Street.

The Food Cougar home office in Hattiesburg gave their stressed young manager a mandatory two-week "vacation" and politely suggested professional counseling. They arranged a session with the company psychiatrist. Mark stood by his story and continued to believe people had sex on his potato display. No one else believed him. He took advantage of the paid two-week vacation, then told Food Cougar to shove it!

"I don't need a psychiatrist. I need a new career." Mark thought selling cars would be an interesting, stress-free change of pace.

14

IT TOOK NEARLY TWENTY YEARS for the Mississippi Gulf Coast to recover from Hurricane Camille. The hurricane had 200-mile-per-hour winds and a twenty-five-foot storm surge. For decades most Gulf Coast property contained vacant, cement slabs of destroyed structures. There was no economic incentive to rebuild or develop anything significant. There were a few Waffle Houses and fast-food outlets, not much more. A large deep-water fishing boat was pushed a block inland by Camille's surge. It was converted into a tourist gift shop and stayed rusting away in the same spot for years. Then the casinos came to town. Now much of the Mississippi coast looked like Las Vegas. The economic activity had been helpful. It was nice to have good restaurants and hotels.

Although the Mississippi Gulf Coast offered many good restaurant choices, Andre decided to do something really special. Saint Ann's was located midway between the Mississippi Gulf Coast and New Orleans. Driving to the Crescent City would take about the same time. Vincent's on Saint Charles Avenue was one of the best Italian restaurants in New Orleans. Located on the streetcar line a few blocks from Tulane University, lunch here was an event to remember.

Mr. Gains and Mr. Richard would have been happy at Burger King. Anything was better than Saint Ann's baloney sandwiches again. Everyone sat at a round table near the back of the restaurant. Vincent's offered an incredible selection of lobster, steak, seafood, prime rib, and specialty dishes. Andre ordered escargot, turtle soup, and the eggplant seafood medallions. The eggplant was sliced and stacked in layers. Between each layer was a stuffing made with shrimp and crabmeat. The entire entrée was covered with a wine and mushroom sauce. The head chef said it was "a classic French dish."

Mr. Gains and Mr. Richard were overwhelmed by the variety.

"You can make as many selections as you like. Try everything," Andre suggested.

"Even prime rib? Andre, are you sure this is okay?" Mr. Richard asked again before getting up from the table. Mr. Gains and Mr. Richard stepped outside to watch a streetcar pass.

While they were away, Lesley stated what Clarence and Andre already knew. "We can't bring them back to Saint Ann's." Clarence reminded them that he had two unused and furnished bedrooms. Lesley hugged his neck.

"You're wonderful. I love you so much!" She kissed him.

You can learn a lot about people from watching them eat. Mr. Richard unfolded his red cloth napkin and carefully placed it on his lap. He arranged his utensils in progression from small to large. He used the correct soup spoon. He knew which glass of water was his. He carefully placed a small pat of butter on his bread dish. The waiter asked if he wanted a refill on his sweet tea. Mr. Richard waved his right hand over the top of the glass. "No thank you." He cut a single bite of prime rib, then set his knife across the upper edge of his plate, with the serrated blade edge facing toward him. Mr. Richard held his fork the same way you hold a pencil. He took his time, enjoying each bite. Repeating the process, he closed his eyes before swallowing.

"It's been a long time since I enjoyed a meal like this," Mr. Richard said. "This cut of prime rib was better than Louis the Fourteenth's. It was a Washington DC restaurant on the first floor of the Watergate complex. I was once a regular there," he said.

Mr. Richard had been a political analyst for the Competitive Enterprise think tank. A PhD from Princeton in Comparative Politics qualified him as lead analyst for Japan, China, Eastern Russia, Siberia, Asia, and the Philippines. His first published work, *The Politics of Oil*, was studied by policymakers and elected officials of the Democratic Party and condemned by Republicans. He was often quoted in international policy journals and Washington briefings. Mr. Richard enjoyed the recognition and prestige of his important job.

"But the stress was unbearable."

On multiple occasions his congressional testimony helped shape national policy decisions. He advised congress during the Tiananmen Square events in China and during multiple South China Sea diplomatic brush-ups. The Defense Department sought his counsel when considering the closure of Clark and Subic Bay bases in the Philippines. When the Soviet Union collapsed, the Energy Department sought his counsel regarding Siberian and Mongolian energy deposits.

"There is no right or wrong, only opinion. Many powerful people disagreed with my views," he said.

Richard quoted words written by Dante 700 years ago. "Midway through the journey of my life I came to a dark wood where the path had been lost." His second nervous breakdown occurred at age forty-seven. Mr. Richard spent thirty-five consecutive days in a mental health residential facility affiliated with Walter Reed Hospital.

"We sat in circles discussing our feelings. I took a cupful of pills five times a day," he said. "At about that same time, I suspected my wife of having an affair. She was attending an out-of-town convention. I drove through the night, arriving at the convention center later the next day. Planning to confront the lovers, I waited in the hotel lobby. The lovebirds exited the elevator arm in arm, kissing each other like honeymooners. I was prepared for anything except the fact that her lover was a friend of mine," he said.

Richard tried various low-stress jobs, including writing a book, but "my nerves are completely shot. I stayed home watching TV and inhaling secondhand smoke. That is when my emphysema problems started."

"How did you get down South?" Clarence asked.

Mr. Richard did not want his enemies to have the satisfaction of seeing him in this defeated condition. "Political enemies are for keeps. They want you destroyed professionally and personally. That way they never need to worry about you reappearing as a threat. They won. I moved south. Out of sight, out of mind. I didn't want to give them the satisfaction, so I ran away!"

He had been on Social Security disability benefits and heavy medication since then. His disability checks went directly to his wife. "She pays Saint Ann's twelve hundred dollars a month and keeps the rest. She is screwing around with her live-in twenty-eight-year-old Algerian lover. She tells everyone her friend is a foreign exchange student. My wife won't ever divorce me. If she does she loses access to my benefits. So here I am." He raised both hands with his palms up as a sign of capitulation.

He added that he liked Saint Ann's because "everyone there is unloved, unwanted, and forgotten. I fit in."

After the meal they enjoyed bread pudding with a dark roast coffee and chicory blend. Andre asked Mr. Gains about the 1959 Mack Parker events in Poplar Grove. Mr. Gains explained everything in great detail. Andre asked him many questions and was impressed with Mr. Gains' intellect and ability to remember dates and details with clarity.

"All I know for certain is that the mob leader was known as Scalper. But no one has ever been willing to identify him," he explained.

He also maintained a great sense of humor. He said he purchased ginkgo biloba tablets, "a daily herbal supplement that supports mental alertness and memory strength. But I can't remember to take them!" He laughed.

Andre also asked Clarence and Lesley to tell him everything they could about George Graves. "The smallest detail can be extremely important." He encouraged them to think and then think some more. Lesley did remind them that Spencer was some type of poll watcher working for the Pearl River County Clerk of Court back then.

"He was just a punk driving around in a pickup with a bunch of thugs in the back. He is proud of this," she said.

"The FBI has reopened many of the segregation era hate crime investigations. They have had only modest success. It has been a very long time. It remains unlikely that new evidence or new witnesses will turn up at this point," Andre said, trying to lower expectations. "On the other hand, someone may know something or have evidence not previously disclosed. People change over time. They may talk now. But it is not likely we will find new physical evidence after all these years. Unless someone is really dumb and saved murder evidence as some type of trophy. We will take a look."

15

THE POPLAR GROVE MASONIC LODGE moved to their new location near the highway about fifteen years earlier. Their old original three-story lodge building on Jackson Avenue was built before the Civil War by a wealthy town merchant. He secretly kept five slaves, two women and three men, imprisoned in the basement. They were accused of talking with other slaves belonging to different masters, speaking to the merchant in "insulting terms," and inciting trouble. He branded the slaves with the fleur-de-lis, identifying them as disobedient.

The merchant chained the five to the cold basement walls and floor with heavy iron bands fastened around their necks, ankles, and waists. The iron collars cut into their flesh, creating terrible wounds. They were discovered when the fire department arrived to extinguish a small fire. The merchant told the firemen to "mind their own damn business" when they asked if any people were still in the building. The slaves said they had been in the basement for months, unable to move or change positions, and they were beaten repeatedly with wooden clubs and whips.

Recently the building was sold to The Riverside Academy, a private elementary and secondary school located southeast of town on the Wolf River. The school used the first floor for administration offices and rented the others. The building was an old brick design with a cement veneer facade, two large Greek columns, and windows on the first and second floors. All of the Masonic emblems, including the cornerstone, were transferred to the new location.

The top floor of the old building was now used as a property and casualty insurance office that employed six people. The office was always closed by 5:30 and was not open on weekends. The building's first floor was used by the school. Their employees showed up on a sporadic basis, usually for planning meetings. They did not use this location for students or classrooms. For the past ten years the secluded old basement had been secretly used by the Poplar Grove swingers club. The other employees in the building had no idea! They thought "swingers" was a baseball or golf group.

The building's front exterior door opened to a foyer with three separate interior doors. The first door led to steps heading up to the insurance office. The doorbell button was broken. The second door opened directly to the school offices. The third door had a coded lock device attached to the knob. A small brass pineapple was mounted upside down above the threshold. This door opened to a long staircase leading down to the basement. The stairs were lit with strands of tiny white Christmas tree lights wrapped around the banisters. With no windows the quiet old basement was perfect.

Five rooms, each with beds, couches, and two rocking chairs, were to the right of the long basement hallway. Some people said rocking chairs were made for lovers. The rockers needed to be heavy and strong like those sold at Cracker Country restaurants. Swingers seemed to enjoy rockers the most. There were no doors on any rooms. Rows of comfortable theater-type couches were arranged strategically along the hallway for those who liked to watch. The fifth room was called the "Playroom." A sign read, "Occupancy 20." It still had the Civil War era heavy iron rings and old chains mounted into the thick cement walls. Swingers added fur-lined handcuffs. Lower mounted rings and chains were now used to keep legs spread apart.

In the very back was a large open area with a concert grand piano, leather couches, chairs, and a dance floor. A well-stocked bar was behind the piano. The bartenders dressed as undertakers from the

1870s, with black suits and tall black hats. Beer was iced down in a child-sized casket with silver handles.

Against the far wall was an elaborate antique iron casket with an oval glass window used for viewing in the days before modern embalming techniques allowed for open caskets. Placing flowers on the coffin was considered good luck. But superstitious swingers avoided looking inside the window. Sex is a primal expression of life in its most natural form. Making love on or near the casket was erotic because it was like cheating fate. It's the same reason young lovers sneak into cemeteries. The coffin was there as a reminder to enjoy the day, carpe diem.

Swingers appreciate the wonderful complexities of life more than most people. They are also mindful of the temporary nature of every-thing, especially pleasures of the flesh. Most of the local swingers had memorized the inscription below the casket window, "Seize the day. You may never get the chance to embark on such an adventure again." Every generation, including this one, yields to the next.

The kitchen was used to prepare appetizers. On the countertop was a glass bowl used to hold Viagra tablets. These pills came from a bootleg pharmacy in Matamoros, Mexico, and were purchased in large quantities. The Mexican Viagra was cheap and delivered to Poplar Grove overnight. Behind the kitchen was a fire exit that led up to a parking lot behind the building. On the back wall was a framed poster reminding everyone that following all rules guaranteed an "upscale lifestyle experience":

1)   Must be twenty-one.

2)   Use alcohol in moderation.

3)   No means no.

4)   Everyone must be clean and well groomed.

5)   Respect all members. Participation is always encouraged but never required.

6)   Absolutely no drugs.

7)   Masks and disguises must be worn at all times.

The most important step to solving any mystery is to figure out finances first. Andre was puzzled by the apparent wealth of the Poplar Grove swingers club. But with time it all became clear as day. The Riverside Academy was founded in 1972 as a segregation academy. These schools were common throughout the south as white families fled the desegregating public school systems of the day. Now the schools were called "independent." They had their own organization and accrediting agency, lending a degree of credibility to their questionable origins.

Middle-class Poplar Grove families paid high Riverside tuition and fees, but their children still ended up at Pearl River College with the same black students they tried to avoid. Andre and Clarence didn't understand how these tuition expenses were worthwhile. Riverside had never placed a single child in any private university like Tulane or Vanderbilt. Some Riverside alumni attended the University of Southern Mississippi. Last year their top graduate flunked out of Southern Mississippi and was now back at Pearl River College with everyone else.

This actually worked in Riverside's favor. If their students applied for admission to competitive universities, the families would realize how poorly prepared their graduates were. Since the students all attended open admission colleges, no one was held accountable for the dreadful Riverside academics.

Spencer had been president of the Riverside Board of Directors for the past twelve years. Most of the other school board members were swingers also. They agreed to purchase the old Masonic building with the intent of secretly using the basement for the swingers club. Most of the club's expenses were filtered through the school's budget. Nearly all school budget expense items listed as miscellaneous were actually swinger expenses covered by Riverside parent tuition payments, including the Masonic building rent.

Vidalia onions are only grown in certain parts of Georgia around Glennville. The onions are so sweet, people eat them like apples. Sweet onions are grown in other parts of the country, but they are not Vidalia. Spencer knew that people would pay a premium for the world's best onions. For the past seven years he had organized a Vidalia Onion Fundraiser for the benefit of Riverside Academy.

The fundraiser was "for our children," he always said.

The onions were sold in five-pound sacks. Each student was expected to sell at least ten sacks. Except that Spencer ordered these sweet onions from a farm in Ohio. He changed the labels from Ohio to Georgia and doubled the price. The profits supported swinger events.

Interesting young couples were offered good jobs at the school if they agreed to swing. It was a condition of employment. As a precaution all Riverside employees were offered only single-year contracts. If they didn't swing, the employment contracts were not renewed. The grand piano in the swingers club was purchased with funds from the Riverside band and music program.

16

RUSSELL WAS TOLD ABOUT THE swingers club by Spencer. Lesley did not tolerate that type of behavior. She would never go, but did not care enough anymore to try and stop Spencer. Russell invited a beautiful LSU senate intern and her three friends as his special guests, one for the governor, one for John, one for himself, and one for Spencer. John's supermarkets were facing bankruptcy, but he could still be counted on for large campaign donations.

Russell planned to dress the girls in Catholic schoolgirl uniforms with plaid skirts and saddle oxford shoes. The men would be disguised in black robes and hoods like Franciscan priests. New Orleans Mardi Gras masks were flesh-colored, with round eye holes, small holes for the nose, and an oval cut out for the mouth. Russell cut the entire bottom portion off each mask. They still hid the identity of the wearer but were more comfortable to use, especially during oral sex.

The four girls were waiting at Russell's private hangar, adjacent to the Baton Rouge Regional Airport terminal. "Wheels down. The eagle has landed," his pilot radioed the control tower as Russell returned from Poplar Grove on schedule. All the girls were beautiful, but one was exceptional. Russell had never seen eyes so blue. He thought she had an Eastern European look. But, he was told, the girls were from Leesville in Vernon Parish. Her name was Alexi but her friends called her Alison.

Baton Rouge politicians especially liked hiring interns from this area. Leesville was home to the Fort Polk army base. The town had a population of about six thousand residents. Twenty thousand army recruits were stationed on the base—the fifth largest military installation in the nation. Politicians figured any good-looking college-age girls from this area would already be well "broken in." It was ironic that Leesville was firmly in the Bible Belt. Most residents were Baptist or Pentecostal.

For the most part, the four girls seemed excited about flying in Russell's private plane and about meeting the Louisiana governor. "Is this really your airplane? Do you really know the governor? Are we really invited to a costume party?" Russell answered "yes, yes, yes" to everything. Their cattiness annoyed him. The girls took photos before boarding. The last two digits of the airplane's tail identification numbers, "PT—Papa Tango," were visible in their photos.

A single row of seats faced forward on the plane's left side. Double seats faced each other on the right side of the cabin. Someone had to sit facing backward. Russell always sat in the forward-facing seat on the right. The girls played with the circular sun screens on each window and the round air vents. They loved the comfortable leather seats.

"These are just like the seats in my dad's new Buick. Except his are dark brown."

Russell overheard the girl's whispered comments. "Young lady, each seat in this airplane is individually insured for eight thousand dollars," he said. Then he thought for a minute. "Sweetheart, you are right. They are just like Buick."

She smiled back. "I know. I know. How strange is that? Maybe this airplane is made by Buick."

"Perhaps it is," Russell said.

"By the way, why are we having a costume party? It's not even Halloween, silly," the same girl asked.

The beautiful blue-eyed girl was especially quiet. Alexi seemed unimpressed, like she had been in private airplanes before. Unlikely, considering the economic climate in Vernon Parish, Russell thought. She intrigued him. He liked Alexi the most.

Russell offered drinks from the aircraft's well-stocked bar.

"Do we need IDs?" the girl on his left asked with a concerned and disappointed look. Russell had assumed his guests were all at least twenty-one years old. The college intern was seated across from him and began opening and closing her legs. It was obvious she shaved.

"Do we really need IDs?" she asked in a mischievous way.

What the hell, Russell thought to himself and did not ask about age again.

The intern requested a fifth of peppermint-flavored rum. She drank directly from the bottle and then passed it back and forth to the others. Russell drank three consecutive Maker's Mark doubles on the rocks.

The quiet blue-eyed girl, Alexi, was not actually from Vernon Parish, Louisiana, at all. She was born in Houston. Her daddy, Pavel Navalny, owned the largest independent oil and gas exploration company in Texas. He had other significant multinational interests as well. For the past eight years *Fortune* magazine had named him among the world's wealthiest individuals. He was a single dad and wanted to protect Alexi forever but knew she needed freedom as well. Alexi attended the Kinkaid School in Houston, one of America's most exclusive independent high schools.

The Navalny family purchased a vacation home in Vernon Parish for the hiking, bike paths, and Toledo Bend fishing. Hodges Gardens was located nearby. It was similar to Longue Vue in New Orleans and Bellingrath Gardens in Mobile, Alabama. The beautiful gardens offered peace, tranquility, and escape from their stressful lives. The Navalnys were Christian Orthodox and considered Easter to be the holiest day of the year. Mrs. Navalny loved the Easter Sunday sunrise service held in the gardens each year. She enjoyed long walks in the gardens with Alexi at her side.

The remoteness of the area offered security and seclusion. Yet, it was a short helicopter flight from the family's Houston headquarters. At a cost of ten million dollars, the Augusta Westland AW139 was one of the most expensive civilian helicopters available. Built in the United Kingdom, it had two Pratt and Whitney engines generating 1531 horsepower. It sat ten and had a range of 570 miles at nearly 200 miles per hour.

The very close Navalny family spent summers in Vernon Parish for the past six years. Over that time Alexi had made trusted local friends; some now attended LSU. Her protective dad reluctantly agreed to an unsupervised Baton Rouge visit. Alexi celebrated her seventeenth birthday a month earlier and had never been in trouble or dated a serious boyfriend. She planned to attend Yale University in the fall.

Mr. Navalny was born dirt poor in the town of Astana in Kazakhstan. At the time of the Soviet collapse, he was a low-level, unremarkable worker at a refinery in a dirty industrial town. Communist state-owned enterprises were turned over to private ownership in a disorganized free-for-all. Mr. Navalny went from being a loyal communist refinery worker to a captain of capitalist industry in three short years. He recognized the role of politics in business and became effective at co-opting politicians. With politicians in his back pocket, he made bigger and bigger deals.

"The world changes. We must change along with it," he said.

His Texas company, Circle Hammer Exploration, employed nearly 800 people and operated wells, production platforms, and pipelines crisscrossing the Gulf of Mexico. A Houston newspaper editorial said, "Don't be fooled by his charming demeanor. Pavel Navalny is a ruthless and dangerous 'beeznessman' who left Russia under a murder investigation cloud involving the suspicious death of a former business partner." The unfortunate partner turned up at the bottom of a frozen lake. All charges were dropped after local investigators classified the death as an unfortunate ice-fishing accident.

Another two people were killed when Mr. Navalny's Bentley ran onto the sidewalk of an outdoor café. The unfortunate deaths of two British businessmen were also ruled an accident. Mr. Navalny sent flowers.

In Siberia Mr. Navalny built an expensive but unnecessary power plant, producing overpriced electricity in an area with declining electricity demand. The resulting escalating electricity prices provoked street protest, riots, and the eventual downfall of the corrupt local government. In the town of Rogun, in dirt-poor Tajikistan, Mr. Navalny planned to build a 335-meter-high hydroelectric dam on the Vakhsh River. The proposed cost was more than $7.6 billion. He claimed the electricity could be sold to China. The project angered neighboring nations concerned about water shortages. They halted gas shipments and construction material to Tajikistan. The dam was never finished. Large-scale Russian corruption and criminal activity by oligarchs like Mr. Pavel Navalny had made economic development impossible in that part of the world. "Mr. Navalny toys with nations the way a cat plays with mice," according to the editorial.

Pavel was an expert Preferans player—a Russian card game that resembled bridge. In the Russian game, players made bids or contracts for how many tricks they would take. Other players tried to win tricks away from the top bidder. They hoped to make the bidder come up short on his contracts. Mr. Navalny always won. "In cards and in life, he is always the winning bidder."

The king of Saudi Arabia and the president of Russia were afraid to anger him. Texans were afraid Pavel was bringing bad Russian habits to Texas. His intimidating armed guards were former Russian and Ukraine Special Forces. Regardless of how well they dressed, private armies were unnecessary on the streets of Houston.

But Mr. Navalny had a soft side. He was a protective dad. After his wife's untimely death, he became more protective. Mr. Navalny loved his daughter, Alexi, more than anything.

Mr. Navalny's beautiful wife died after a short illness. She contracted Vibrio Vulnificus from eating raw oysters harvested from

Galveston Bay. Paul was in Eastern Europe and did not make it back to her side. Two days after consuming the oysters, she felt ill with chills and nausea. She was admitted to a Houston hospital with a fever of 102.

"I think I have food poisoning and feel really bad." She asked Paul when he would return home.

Not realizing the severity of her illness, he promised to hurry home but had a few remaining meetings to attend. She was transferred to the hospital's Intensive Care Unit and died within thirty-six hours. The best Houston doctors were unable to save her. Paul promised to always protect Alexi and raise her to be a gracious and kind woman, like her mother. Alexi looked just like her.

17

THE LOUISIANA SECRETARY OF HEALTH and
Hospitals controlled a budget that was one-third of the state's entire
operating finances. The department was responsible for Medicaid,
Behavioral Health, Public Health, Health Information Technology,
Developmental Disabilities, and Aging. Additionally, the secretary
had direct oversight of the Louisiana Hospital Standards Board and
was responsible for health care facility licensure.

Legal fees involved with the initial license of a single hospital or
nursing home could involve over a million dollars. Thereafter, annual
operating profits were at least that much and were a reliable source of
long-term campaign donations. Louisiana politicians used campaign
donations like a legal protection racket. Any facility not paying its
"assessment" could face surprise inspections and closure and fines.

A central Louisiana hospital administrator was investigated for
allegedly giving the governor two hundred thousand dollars cash in a
brown paper bag. The legal limit for cash donations was one thousand
per individual. "We passed the hat around. Twenty doctors gave a
thousand each. Nothing illegal here," he claimed. The state attorney
general, also a friend of the governor, agreed and dismissed the com-
pliant.

"Nothing illegal here," the attorney general echoed. He also complimented the administrator on operating a well-run facility.

The fraudulent issue of state licenses for approving new health care facilities was a profitable endeavor. The Secretary of the Department of Health and Hospitals was appointed by and served at the pleasure of the governor. "Somebody is going to build and operate these facilities. Why shouldn't it be the governor's friends?" the DHH secretary recently asked.

Before they finished dinner at Vincent's, Andre's staff already had a handle on the most important issues. Saint Ann's was listed as an SFF—Special Focus Facility—because of its record of inadequate care. Only a handful of Medicare and Medicaid centers nationwide received this poor classification. Saint Ann's had more safety and injury problems and patterns of serious problems persisting for a long time than nearly any other center in the state.

According to Andre's staff,Recently two residents fell from their wheelchairs. One died from a fractured neck. The other broke his collarbone when he fell against a dresser. Neither wheelchair had anti-tipping safety devices in place. A seventy-year-old female resident died from complications related to bedsores. The sores were the worst we have ever seen. She stayed in the same position for a very long time.

"A cerebral palsy patient was found dead in his room. He had been dead for two days before the body was discovered. In another case of neglect, a stroke patient had difficulty feeding himself and could not indicate when he was thirsty. The untrained Saint Ann's staff had no record of his fluid intake. He died of dehydration. It was a very slow and painful death.

"Last summer a dementia patient in her hospital gown and slippers was found dead on Saint Ann's roof. With no shade the temperatures reached a hundred that day. Her body was discovered by an air-conditioner repairman one week later. The staff did not realize she was missing because they put someone else in her room by mistake. They offered no explanation. The family was told the patient died peacefully in her sleep."

Lesley, Clarence, Mr. Gains, and Mr. Richard were surprised by the level of neglect. "Andre, how does this place manage to stay open?" Lesley shook her head in disbelief.

"It's all very sad," Mr. Gains added.

"There is much more. We have multiple pages of incidents just like this."

Andre asked his staff to research all records of Saint Ann's license inspections, health department inspections, and names of every state inspector who ever set foot there. He wanted to know everything possible about Saint Ann's licensing process. Most important, he wanted to know who owned it. Andre directed his staff like a general commanding an army.

"Always follow the money," Mr. Richard said in agreement.

Researching ownership of Louisiana licensed hospitals and assisted living facilities should have been a simple matter of checking public records, but it was never that easy. Ownership was usually hidden behind front companies and multiple layers of overlapping corporations and boards. True owners were always protected from liability by a maze of legal dead-ends. But Andre's staff was efficient at forensic accounting and decoding corporate ownership puzzles. They were already two steps ahead.

"The owner of Saint Ann's operates an umbrella corporation called American Community Care Centers, LLC. Together with various corporations and partners, he owns a total of fifteen nursing homes and has interests in three Louisiana hospitals. He operates the facilities near Louisiana state lines. He can attract out-of-state residents from Arkansas, Texas, and Mississippi while being regulated by corrupt Louisiana bureaucrats. That is why Saint Ann's is located so close to Poplar Grove, Mississippi. The owner is a member of the governor's inner circle of most trusted friends. He is involved in everything from educational software and streetcar lines to hospitals. His name is Russell Burley."

18

ALTHOUGH SPENCER WAS ENTHUSIASTIC about the swingers event that evening, he tried hard to concentrate and put business first. The job interview would take only a few minutes. He added three or four rookies to his sales force each year. New hires could be expected to last about four months before washing out. Usually this was a first job for the new salesmen. Most held two-year associate degrees in marketing from Pearl River College but had no real sales training. Spencer had been recognized by the college for hiring recent grads. They said he was "a good corporate citizen and strong role model."

Occasionally the new hires were older, having washed out at other jobs. Regardless, Spencer paid a one-thousand-dollar draw per month. The salesmen earned no commissions until the monthly draw was covered. Most never earned enough in commission to cover the stipend, and once they finally gave up and quit, they usually owed Spencer thousands of dollars. The signed employment contract was legally enforceable. Spencer had seized assets and garnished wages from failed salesmen.

New hires started out with enthusiasm, making cold calls, knocking on doors, and running newspaper ads. Occasionally a car was actually sold. But once the rookie quit, Spencer divided that prospect list with his senior salesmen. The real salesmen worked the leads, made sales, and generated thousands in commissions.

Being proud of the promising new career path, parents and grand-parents could always be counted upon to show up and buy a new or used car. Spencer raised the price on these easy sales because he knew the happy family would gladly pay full sticker without question, especially when they believed they were helping build success. But Spencer posted the additional revenue to price, not commission. The profits went directly to the dealership's bottom line. Family sales did little to cover the new salesmen's salary draw.

Mark's first interview at Spencer's dealership was scheduled at three on Saturday afternoon with Mr. Robert. Mark took advantage of Food Cougar's two weeks' paid vacation and spent the time sleeping late and reading self-improvement books. He did not keep the appointment with Food Cougar's company psychiatrist. "I don't need any shrink to tell me what I saw on my potato display," he said.

Mark was ready to start a real career with a supportive employer, doing something he actually enjoyed. If things went well with Mr. Robert's interview, then he would be meeting Spencer. Mark's mother was proud that her son had an appointment with the mayor of Poplar Grove. "You are already successful in my book," she said and gave him a kiss on the cheek for good luck. "I'm so proud," she added. If everything went well, Mark hoped to start a new career as a car salesman Monday morning.

Mark purchased a button-down collar shirt and colorful tie from the DC Dirt Cheap Boutique. He did not own a sport coat but planned to wear a dark windbreaker instead. Mark spent Saturday morning washing his car and cleaning out the interior. He got a haircut and polished his shoes with KIWI shoe polish he purchased from the drugstore. He reviewed his resume and stood in front of the mirror practicing his initial greeting and answers to expected interview questions.

"I appreciate the opportunity. I appreciate the opportunity to interview with this very fine organization. Thank you, sir," he repeated over and over again, hoping to get his introduction just right.

Mark expected to be asked about the abrupt ending to his Food Cougar career. He did not have a good answer for that. It probably would be a bad idea to mention the company shrink situation or the in-store sex. Maybe he could blame everything on long hours, poor pay, and stress. Better yet, he could just say he decided to move on and pursue better opportunities at an outstanding company "like this." These better opportunities would allow him to afford night classes at the University of Southern Mississippi in Hattiesburg. A four-year degree in political science was within reach if Mark received credit for all the community college work he'd completed. Then law school could be a real possibility.

He arrived fifteen minutes early but did not expect to see two other job applicants also waiting to see Mr. Robert. The receptionist introduced herself and asked his name.

"You're on the list. The three of you will see Mr. Robert in a few minutes. Good luck," Melissa said with a flirtatious smile.

"Do we all interview together?" Mark was confused.

The other two candidates were older—well dressed in expensive suits and carrying real leather briefcases. He felt intimidated and thought about leaving.

"Right this way. Mr. Robert is ready." Melissa escorted the applicants to a small conference room usually used for closing car deals. "Mr. Robert will be right in. Please have a seat."

Robert placed a small plastic model of a 1957 Thunderbird convertible on the conference table. It was red with a white interior and black convertible top. "I want each of you to sell this Thunderbird model to me." Mr. Robert leaned back in his chair and pointed to the first person to his right. "Let's start with you."

Mark was surprised by the man's shaking hands and perspiring forehead.

"Start with me!" He seemed ready to panic. "Soooo, this is a Ford Thunderbird model. It is made of high-quality plastic with great attention paid to every detail." He paused to dab a handkerchief on his forehead.

"The doors, hood, and trunk all open. The engine compartment is exactly like the original car." Mr. Robert was unimpressed. "The convertible top will fold down, exposing the realistic-looking interior." He held the model out for everyone to see as he demonstrated the top movement. "This model sells for a reasonable price of thirty-five dollars." The salesman sat down.

"Get the fuck out of here. You are wasting my time." Mr. Robert pointed to the man sitting next to Mark. "Your turn."

The next job applicant was much more collected and polished. He delivered a similar presentation, discussing the attributes of the plastic model. Mr. Robert was looking out the window, daydreaming. His Lincoln was parked nearby.

"The '57 Thunderbird was Ford's first attempt to compete with Chevrolet's successful Corvette sports car."

Mark knew 1955 was the first year for the two-seater Thunderbird, not 1957.

"How can you sell a product if you don't know the product?" Mr. Robert asked. "Get out of here!"

Mark stood up and rolled the Thunderbird across the table. "You bought a big Lincoln sedan because that is what everyone expected. It is a true status symbol. You have arrived! You are financially successful! The Nimitz-class Lincoln makes you feel important, but it won't make you happy." Mr. Robert enjoyed the clever aircraft carrier comparison. Mark had his attention. "The sedan is for business. This convertible is for you!"

Mark folded the convertible top down and placed the Thunderbird directly in front of Mr. Robert. "Imagine a warm spring day. You are driving with the top down, heading to Key West for a long weekend. The sun is high in a blue sky. Your wife leans her head back, enjoying the sultry breeze through her hair. She has never looked more beautiful, in her tiny red bikini and white sunglasses. She glances in your direction. You enjoy seeing her smile. The powerful Thunderbird accelerates past beaches and ocean, a magic carpet taking you away." Mark took his seat.

Robert looked at the Thunderbird and said nothing for a long moment. "I want you to meet the mayor."

Spencer was in a hurry. "I'm happy to meet you, young man. Robert likes you and so do I. You have the job."

Mark and Spencer shook hands. Mark knew this was also a test. He did not let go first. "Oh! You are good!" Spencer said with a big smile. "I have a very important commitment this evening. Need to run! See you Monday morning." As he was leaving Spencer asked Melissa for one of his signed photos. He handed it to Mark. "This is for you."

"Make sure you sign all the salary paperwork. The employment contract is most important. We will handle everything else, including salary and dress code discussions, on Monday. Welcome aboard," Robert said as he escorted Mark to the front door.

19

A MAN WAS SITTING IN a metal chair near the front door leading to the basement. The chair was leaning against the wall on two legs. The man was about halfway through a paperback book about jazz great Miles Davis. The lighting was poor. He showed almost no interest in the many unusual swingers parading past his vantage point.

Everyone said, "Good evening, Mr. Fatso."

The man's real name was William, but the secret code for tonight's get-together was "Mr. Fatso." He pressed a concealed button, opening the door. William was a fullback for the Wildcats. After college he enlisted in the Marines and was still strong and fit. The small .22 caliber handgun he always carried was for "personal protection." Mr. Fatso considered the five hundred dollars cash he would earn this evening to be easy money.

Mr. Fatso had seen pirates and wenches wearing booty shorts, pajamas, pasties, and many fantasy fashions. Some guests were formal and looked like they were planning a night at the symphony and dinner at Commander's Palace. But another group arrived as the naughty school reunion. There was the principal, the school nerd, the cheerleader, the jock, the schoolgirl, the nurse, and the coach. A big man with a beard and hairy chest arrived dressed in a pink ballet tutu. Mr. Fatso looked up for a minute.

"It's all right, my brother. It's all right," he said and went back to his Miles Davis book after pressing the button.

There were many togas. A woman showed up with a three-foot inflatable penis strapped to her. It hung out from under her toga. She tied a green neon light ring around its head. Mr. Fatso thought it looked like a radioactive mushroom. Another couple arrived dressed in business attire. He had an inflatable female sex doll belted to his waist in the sixty-nine position. She carried a male doll the same way.

In the first room one rocking chair was being used, and three young couples were playing undressing games in the bed. Two women sitting on the couch watched everything. Caressing each other's breasts, they kissed. Three men standing nearby encouraged them. "Please don't stop there," they pleaded. The room's only light was provided by two candles in sconces mounted on the back wall. A man sat in the first rocker dressed in a tuxedo. His black-and-white Phantom of the Opera mask covered half his face. His pants were unbuttoned and unzipped.

A middle-aged woman in a toga stood over the Phantom. Her legs were apart and inviting. Her husband was behind her. He placed his hands on her shoulders, sliding her toga off. It fell in waves around her ankles. She had firm breasts and erect nipples that pointed slightly upward. Her legs were strong. There was an unusual tattoo on her left cheek with the number 335. She reached down to the Phantom's thighs and gently tugged his pants down. Aroused, he tripled in size. She glanced back at her husband, seeking approval. He kissed her on the cheek.

"It's okay," he whispered in her ear, offering encouragement.

She sat on top. Her legs were wrapped over the arms of the rocker. The chair's movement helped stimulate her in unusual and unfamiliar ways. She loved the repetitive in-and-out motion. It was the most intense climax she had ever experienced.

"We need to buy a Cracker rocker," her husband said after his wife's first encounter of the evening ended.

The three playful couples in the bed each took turns removing items of clothing from each other. They were giggling and throwing pants and shirts around the room. The woman closest to the head of the bed sat up and was first to pull her pink thong underwear down. She was a natural redhead.

Once she had everyone's attention, she pulled the thong back up. "No, no, no," she said in a firm but friendly voice while playfully moving her index finger back and forth like she's scolding some disobedient pet. Unable to resist the teasing, a man lying on his back pulled her down on top of him.

"What took you so long?" she asked. After a few minutes they all switched positions again.

A woman dressed as a college coed approached the other Cracker rocking chair. She was a high school science teacher at Riverside. Facing backward, she sat on her knees. Raising her skirt, she got into a comfortable position.

"I'm willing to do anything for an A."

Anticipating pleasure, her hands held tight to the top of the chair with her face pressed deep into a feather pillow.

Her friend, dressed as a university professor in a tweed jacket with leather elbow patches, unzipped his pants.

"How bad do you need that passing grade?"

Holding both sides of the chair, he rocked it back and forth aggressively. She guided him into her favorite position. The chair did the rest of the work.

"You're my favorite professor. I love your class even if you are an easy A!"

Other men, hoping to have a turn with the sexy coed, waited quietly for the "professor" to finish. There was no jealousy or romance at swingers events. It was all about sex and more sex.

An older couple, Joe and Clair, sat on a couch near the second bedroom. Clair seemed very uncomfortable. They were in their late fifties and had been drinking regular Coca-Cola. She wore her hair in the wedding cake style of the early 1960s. He was stuffed like a sausage into an Adidas track suit. After years of persistent asking and nagging, this was the first time Clair gave in and agreed to attend a swingers event. She was concerned that she would be recognized by other followers of Brother Love's Baptist flock.

"I am a member of the Vestry Board and Sunday Coffee Committee. I should never be in a place like this."

"Relax. Brother Love is probably somewhere around here himself." Joe told her to take it easy and have another Coke.

A healthy-looking young man happened to sit nearby. He was wearing a Blessed Mother medal on a silver chain. "Do you mind? I don't think my wife has ever seen a Catholic man," Joe remarked in a friendly manner with a wink of his right eye.

"No problem at all," the man happily agreed and took it out.

After a long glance, Clair looked away. "I'm Baptist! I can't look at that. Oh my gosh! Are you crazy?"

Joe asked his wife to stand. She resisted but eventually did as he asked. Joe removed her clothes. Shyly, she covered herself with her hands. Clair was tall and still very attractive. She also had a 335 tattoo. Joe asked her to turn around and commented about her remarkable body.

"Why don't you kiss him?"

"Are you out of your mind?" Clair was worried that the man may be from Poplar Grove's Catholic ghetto. "You want me to put my mouth on that? Is it clean?"

"This is a very nice man," Joe reassured her.

Reluctantly Clair gave it two short kisses and then looked away. Joe turned her head back. This time she did it with enthusiasm. She stopped, took a short breather, then did it again, and again.

"Are you happy? Am I done now?"

"Not quite," Joe said. "I think this nice Catholic man would like to have all of you."

Joe told Clair to sit down on the couch. She complained and said her husband was nuts. She thought his recurring gout had somehow infected his warped brain. "Only a crazy man would want to see his God-fearing Southern Baptist wife with a Catholic man," Clair mumbled under her breath. She continued to protest nonstop but leaned back on the couch anyway, spreading her knees far apart. She gripped the Catholic man with both hands and guided him in.

"You happy now?" she asked Joe. "Oh my gosh! Oh my gosh! Is this how they do it in the Catholic ghettos?" she asked no one in particular.

For a second Joe thought he heard his out-of-breath Baptist wife say, "Give me more! I like Catholic men." She may also have said something unpleasant about Brother Love, but he couldn't be sure. Joe enjoyed watching the contrast of the young Catholic man deep inside his Baptist wife.

"I'm doing this for you! This is for you," Clair said to Joe while changing positions and kissing her new Catholic friend one more time.

"I know you are, baby. I know. You're doing this just for me." Joe enjoyed watching his wife misbehave.

The activities in each of the other rooms were very similar. Most chairs along the hall were occupied with people drinking, flirting, or resting. In the playroom two women were handcuffed to the wall with the fur straps. The cuffed women swayed to loud rock music playing from speakers. At least twenty people were in the middle of the room. The orgy got started with a few couples playing Strip Roulette. The winner of each spin had the right to ask any other player to do whatever they wished. The only rule was that each winner's request had to be more daring than the preceding one. As others joined in, things got really interesting as each wheel spin resulted in multiple winners and losers. Various sexual positions with multiple partners were popular. This game was a favorite swingers icebreaker.

In the back room a few couples were dancing, two people were playing the piano, a few were seated at the bar enjoying small talk. Here and there couples were having sex against the wall. One woman had her hands on the casket. Her partner approached.

"This is kinky but I like it. It's like we are mocking death," she said.

It would be interesting to know what Charles Darwin would think of swingers. Theories of natural selection, incremental evolution, and evolutionary fitness don't seem to apply at swinger events. When everyone is screwing everyone else indiscriminately, gene flow theories of evolution and sexual selection seem disproven. In fact swingers incorporate no selection process at all; everyone screws everyone. Darwin would probably consider them outliers. Even Sigmund Freud would be puzzled by this bunch.

With so much activity going on, it was not surprising at all that no one noticed Russell's group of four monks and four girls in Catholic school uniforms enter just after nine o'clock. In thirty minutes Russell's Mexican Viagra pills would kick in. He planned to keep a close eye on Alexi until then. This time he was not going to share his prize with the governor, Spencer, or anyone else.

20

AFTER THIRTY MINUTES OR SO, the small talk started to die down. The drive from New Orleans to Poplar Grove seemed long, especially after such a wonderful meal. Mr. Gains and Richard were still discussing the politics of the Middle East, although with less and less passion as the miles and minutes rolled along. The Rebirth Jazz band was playing on WWOZ, Clarence's favorite New Orleans FM station. Feeling drowsy Andre pulled over for coffee at the second Slidell Exit. It seemed they had enough gas to make it back to Poplar Grove.

"We will cut it close, but I don't feel much like pumping gas now anyhow." Clarence was asleep.

Lesley leaned against him, snuggling under his right arm. Her eyes were open. She smiled at Andre. He enjoyed seeing Clarence happy.

Forty minutes later the low fuel light warning appeared a few miles outside Poplar Grove. Lesley said she would like to use the restroom anyhow and Clarence agreed. Mr. Gains and Mr. Richard were sleeping like babies. Pulling over, Andre put a credit card in the pump. Clarence stood up straight and then arched his back. He reached high with both arms and made a grizzly bear sound. He offered his hand, helping Lesley out of the car.

"Does he always stretch like that?" Lesley asked while playfully poking Clarence in his ribs.

"At least since the fourth grade that I'm aware of."

She laughed at how well Clarence and Andre knew each other.

Clarence was suddenly serious.

"What is a Dominican high school girl doing out here this time of night?" Clarence asked, pointing to a lonely figure sitting on a small bench under a nearby streetlight.

The unique plaid patterns of the school's uniform were easy to recognize. It was clear she was very upset. She was crying nonstop. Tears streaked down her face. She was missing a shoe and her shirt was torn. Lesley sat next to the young girl.

"Are you okay, sweetheart? Do you need help?"

She tried to speak but was overcome with fear. Her body shook. Lesley hugged her tight until the crying slowed and asked her name.

"Alexi. I'm Alexi Navalny. My daddy is coming. He's on his way." She was trying to catch her breath.

"Where is your daddy now? What about your mother?" Clarence asked in a compassionate tone. He wanted to get his hands on the man who tried to hurt this innocent child.

"He's in Houston. My daddy is in Houston. My mother died a few months ago."

Lesley hugged her tighter and explained to Alexi that Texas was a long way from Poplar Grove, Mississippi, and she couldn't stay at this gas station all night. "Is there someone nearby we can call?" Alexi insisted that her daddy would be there in a few minutes. Lesley invited Alexi to come home with them until her father arrived.

"Let's get you somewhere safe."

Richard said he had written articles about a Pavel Navalny from Eastern Russia. "Couldn't be the same man. Could it?"

All of Pavel Navalny's guards were trained professional killers. They were recruited from the Spetsnaz and Vympel Russian Special Forces. Most served in the 2nd and 16th Spetsnaz Brigades. They were trained in hand combat, underwater combat, parachutes, and urban warfare techniques. In addition to basic Russian Special Forces training, each was also qualified to wear the maroon beret. The closest American equivalent was SEAL Team 6.

To qualify for the beret, each had to complete a twenty-kilometer cross-country run in full combat uniform, a 200-meter sprint, urban assault exercises, a twenty-minute freestyle sparring match against four separate opponents, and a two-week winter survival exercise in Siberia. Only ten percent of all Russian Special Forces passed the tests and wore the beret. Pavel's men wore Armani suits and Italian leather shoes now, but on certain occasions, they still wore the Russian maroon beret.

The one soft spot these dangerous men shared was their love for Alexi. Their first duty was to protect her, but they also helped her learn to ride a bicycle, climb trees, and fish. The driving age in Louisiana was fifteen. They taught her to drive well enough to earn her first learner's permit. The guards helped Alexi with homework, especially Cold War and Soviet Union history. She always got As in these subjects. When she was younger they had been known to play hide-and-seek, kick-the-can, and jump rope. Alexi always won. They attended her childhood make-believe tea parties without complaint. They used to affectionately call her "Poof" because her long hair had a tendency to poof up in damp weather. These dangerous men loved Alexi like a little sister.

At low altitude and 230 miles per hour, the Augusta Westland had already passed Lafayette. The helicopter's official top speed was reported to be 200 mph. On this night that did not matter to Pavel Navalny and his men. He demanded more speed. The aircraft approached 250 mph with the pilots pushing it harder and harder. The interior was lit in an orange glow. The men checked and double-checked their weapons.

"The FAA is demanding that we land now. Evidently we are breaking multiple flight rules. The Americans say we have not filed a flight plan," the co-pilot told Mr. Navalny in Russian, then turned off the radio.

"ETA Poplar Grove Mississippi, forty-three minutes," the pilot announced in a clear, professional voice.

"Hang on, Alexi. We're coming. Just a few more minutes." Pavel wanted Alexi safe in his arms. He also felt rage building inside him. "Who are these men? Who are these men that dare harm my Alexi?"

21

PAVEL'S HELICOPTER LANDED IN THE blueberry field directly across from Clarence's front yard. Pavel ran toward the house before the rotors had a chance to slow down. His men followed close behind. George came out on his front porch with a twelve-gauge shotgun to see what the commotion was about. The Russians told him to go back inside.

"This is not your beezness."

"Fucking right about that." George went inside and turned off all his lights. He wondered what trouble Clarence was involved with. George thought the men were speaking "Colombian." He assumed they were drug dealers from South America.

A Poplar Grove sheriff's patrol car happened by. The patrolman kept photos of his young family taped to his dashboard. Last year he earned thirteen thousand dollars as a patrolman and six thousand dollars working as a bank guard on weekends. The job was not worth his life.

The officer glanced at the helicopter and the numerous heavily armed men running about. He recognized a few of the words they spoke as Russian. Even their English sounded Russian. The police officer spent a year as a US embassy guard in Moscow. He knew that in the Russian language, the letter H was always pronounced as G. In the photo his three-year-old son was swinging a plastic baseball bat at a ball tossed by his gorgeous wife.

Multiple automatic weapons were pointed in his direction. The young policeman was armed with a loaded .38 revolver that he had fired in the line of duty only once. He also had a shotgun in the trunk. The decision was easy. He turned off the blue lights, took his hand off his weapon, put the patrol car in reverse, and backed away. The Russians appreciated his wise decision. They had no issues with him.

Pavel sprinted across Clarence's front yard onto the porch. His manner was intense. He didn't knock.

"I'm sorry, Daddy. I'm so sorry!" Alexi ran into his arms.

He told her repeatedly that everything would be okay. He wiped away her tears. "I knew you would come for me," she said.

"It is not your fault. You are safe now. Daddy loves you always."

Pavel barked orders to his men. "Find them. I want the men that hurt my daughter! " He looked in Andre's direction, recognizing his concern. "Do you have any daughters?" he asked. "Tell me, Counselor." In certain parts of Europe lawyers were often referred to as counselors. "Do you suggest I go to the FBI or the local police? And how will these authorities get my daughter's innocence back?"

Pavel said justice and revenge went together like hammers and nails. But he insisted he was not a killer. He had built more schools than some governments and distributed more polio and malaria vaccines than UN health agencies.

"This is personal. They have taken from my family. Now I must take from them." He called it an eye for an eye, a square deal. "In my country justice is not given. It is taken."

The evening was growing late. Mr. Fatso hoped to be heading home soon. He looked forward to telling his wife about the unique swingers he had seen tonight. He did not notice the three well-dressed men approach until they were already at the front door. They asked about four monks and Catholic schoolgirls.

"I can't allow you to enter unless you know the password. Sorry, gentlemen. That's the rule. You guys are not even in costume. " He hoped his polite manner would discourage any trouble.

They ignored his directions and proceeded toward the stairs. Mr. Fatso stood up, blocking the threshold. "Okay, tough man. You really want a password?" The Russian held a Makarov semiautomatic pistol an inch from Fatso's forehead. "Does this work?"

As a former marine Mr. Fatso knew a real weapon when he saw one. He also knew how professionally trained soldiers handled weapons. They didn't make idle threats. Looking down the short barrel, he could see a bullet in the chamber. The hammer was cocked and the safety was off. He had no doubt this Russian would not hesitate to pull the trigger.

"I don't want any trouble, gentlemen. I ain't seen nothing."

Mr. Fatso decided against pulling out his little 22 pistol. The Russians did not wait for him to press the buzzer. They kicked the door in and proceeded down the stairs. Mr. Fatso picked up his Miles Davis book, calmly walked to his car, and drove away wondering what Russians were doing in Poplar Grove. He wanted to believe the event was just some elaborate sex game hoax. But he knew the semiautomatic pistol was real. His hands began to shake as he realized lives could be at risk.

By this late hour most swingers had already left. But Spencer and John were in the back room leaning against the bar. They were congratulating each other on the evening's success and discussing Russell's Viagra problem. "Where is Russell now?" the Russians asked. Spencer said it was none of their fucking business. He did not think the guns were real. He thought this was just another swingers stunt. John kept quiet. Spencer was hit hard in the mouth with the back end of a pistol. Three of his teeth rattled across the tile floor. He still refused to answer the Russian's questions.

"I don't know anyone named Russell." Spencer tried to wipe the blood from his face with a napkin. "Take it easy. I'm mayor of Poplar Grove."

This time he was punched. The Russian's massive fist looked almost as big as Spencer's face. It struck with the force of a sledgehammer. Spencer fell unconscious to the floor. He looked like a ragdoll. The Russian put his foot on Spencer's face and pointed his semiautomatic at Spencer's chest. He held his left hand open, blocking his face from blood spray if he pulled the trigger. He was already angry about blood splatter on his suit from Spencer's teeth. The Russian looked over in John's direction.

"We have never shot an American politician. You have five seconds or your mayor dies."

John was sweating. "Okay. Okay. Russell left about an hour ago." John said Russell had a bad reaction to Mexican Viagra and alcohol. He was throwing up. Something was wrong with his blood pressure. His face was red as a tomato and his vision was blurry. He had to be helped up the stairs. An icepack was in his pants to ease the pain of a five-hour erection. John said Russell was chasing after his date when he gripped his chest in pain.

"Don't think he had the chance to enjoy his date very much. Russell passed out while chasing her from room to room. She was really playing hard to get. He fell to the floor, drenched in sweat. He sat slumped against a wall. The last time I saw his date, she was running like a jackrabbit up the back fire escape. Haven't seen her since," John said.

"Find that little bitch!" was the last thing John remembered Russell saying.

"Russell has high blood pressure, heart problems, diabetes, and he is overweight. He also drinks like a fish. Taking a handful of bootleg Viagra was not a very good idea," John said.

The Russians picked up Spencer's teeth as a souvenir for Mr. Navalny. John told them everything else he knew about Russell and the governor.

Russell hoped a peaceful soak in his hot tub would help ease his extreme physical discomfort. He turned on the water jets but kept the temperature set on "cool." He listened to Frank Sinatra sing "What are you doing the rest of your life?" His painful erection was now at least six hours old. Each time his heart beat, he thought his penis would explode. His heart was beating very fast. After forty-five seconds he had already counted 135 beats. Russell cursed the swingers.

"Who buys Viagra from Mexico? Fucking swingers!" He poured another glass of Maker's Mark and drank it like a shot.

"Fuck it!" He poured another glass and another, leaned his head back, and tried to clear his head. After six drinks he actually felt somewhat relaxed and sleepy. His guard was down. A freight train could sneak up on him now and he would not notice.

The Russians confirmed the airplane call letters "PT Papa Tango" were registered to a plane owned by Community Care Centers LLC, a corporation owned by Russell Burley. Russell's weak physical condition made the Russians' work that much easier.

Pavel introduced himself to everyone at Clarence's house. He thanked them for helping Alexi.

"We are all family now."

He explained that nothing was more important to him than his daughter. "I am grateful to each of you." Lesley said she did not have children, but if she had a daughter, she hoped she would be sweet like Alexi. Lesley continued to hug Alexi. Pavel stopped before shaking Richard's hand.

"Are you *the* Richard Tower? I have read your books. Great work, but your Russian oil thesis was all wrong. You should call me."

These assassins were not what you would expect. They did not need physical size to intimidate. They looked more like Morgan Stanley bond traders than professional killers. They were surprised how easy it was to hold Russell's head under water. With a hand pushing down on each shoulder, he slipped below the water with little resistance.

The water intake was mounted on the tub's bottom. The suction held Russell down. His face was just a few inches below the water's surface, his eyes open wide. Russell knew it was over. The Russians turned the hot tub temperature settings to the highest levels and disappeared back into the night. Under the circumstances it was unlikely that Russell's death would be considered anything other than an "unfortunate hot tub accident."

Death was a gift for Russell, like a holiday package wrapped and hidden under the tree. The revolving door of too many unpleasant surprises spun like the hands on the face of a clock.

Round and round, we count the minutes and hours, sweeping away days and weeks. Like summer surrendering to fall or the names and faces of half-forgotten lovers unwinding like leaves in autumn, everything must end. Although unpleasant, death can be experienced only once. It is easier than spending years piecing together fragments of a wasteful life.

Death was the best alternative for Russell. Otherwise, Pavel would have destroyed him professionally and personally, taking everything he loved. For the rest of his life, Russell would have wished he was dead.

22

THE RESPONSIBILITY OF TRAINING MARK how to be a successful car salesman fell to Clarence. Spencer unexpectedly decided to take a few weeks off, something about dental work. He was relieved to hear that the county coroner and sheriff found nothing suspicious in Russell's death. It was ruled accidental. Spencer also told the sheriff not to investigate the helicopter landing on Michigan Avenue. He did not want to ever see any more Russians in Poplar Grove.

The paper ran a front-page story about the unexpected forced landing of an offshore oil industry helicopter after mechanical failure. "A Thrilling Night on Michigan Avenue." The article quoted Spencer, "It was a minor mechanical problem with the helicopter. They were back in the air after a few hours."

George told the newspaper reporter they were "armed South American drug dealers." No one believed him.

Spencer asked Lesley to help out at the dealership. Speaking was difficult and painful for him, and managing a few sentences was the best he could do.

"Robert has been acting unusual lately. Really strange. He spends all day looking at ads for old Thunderbirds. Perhaps you could keep an eye on things for the next couple weeks." Spencer told Lesley he fell down the back stairs, knocking out his teeth.

She decided not to ask him how he got a footprint on his face. Spencer believed he could trust Lesley to keep things at the dealership running smoothly. She knew the business well and had worked in most aspects of it over the years.

But he had no idea his wife was in love with someone else and no clue how much she actually despised him. She knew what happened. Lesley was still at Clarence's house comforting Alexi when the Russian bodyguards returned from the swingers party and handed two teeth to Mr. Navalny. This wasn't hard to figure out.

"Lucky you were not killed falling down those steps. You should be more careful," she advised Spencer. "I would love to help. Don't you worry about a thing. Get well, baby." She kissed her fingers and touched them to Spencer's forehead. "Your troubles will melt like lemon drops," she reassured him with her favorite quote from "Somewhere Over the Rainbow."

Lesley was smart and no longer fooled by his manipulative and controlling antics. She was playing Spencer the way Louis Armstrong played the trumpet, with remarkable skill. Lesley could not wait to see Clarence. Her heart raced and her neck blushed. She told Clarence she got goose bumps thinking about him.

Unlike many young people, Mark had a strong work ethic. He was always on time. "I would rather be an hour early than five minutes late," he told Clarence. Mark would work twelve hours a day without complaint if asked. He was always busy, polishing new Fords in the showroom and cleaning windows during slow times. He read the owner's manuals for the new cars and was able to explain the features of each model. Mark liked the Fords and Lincolns but dreamed of polishing his own Jaguar or Maserati. He was always optimistic with a positive outlook.

"This is the best opportunity I've ever had," he said.

Mark explained that he always planned to go to law school, but it just wasn't in the cards. His father had a good job at the paper mill. As shift manager he was earning about forty-five thousand dollars a year. He quit the job three weeks before he left Mark's mother because he did not want to make years of alimony payments.

"I owe that woman nothing. Ain't no court ever going to change that," he told Mark. He had been unemployed and broke ever since.

The family saved seven thousand dollars for Mark's college education. But his father used the money as a down payment to purchase a timber saw. "This saw is a once-in-a-lifetime opportunity," he explained. Mark's dad planned to start his own lumber mill but had no customers or employees, and no timber, investment capital, or business experience. The saw was industrial grade; tree trunks entered one end and finished boards exited the other. It sat unused, rusting in a shed outside of town where it had been hidden from creditors.

Mark's dad now told everyone he managed a small vintage car museum near the town of Wiggins. But the vehicles were unrestored and kept outdoors, unprotected in an open field next to a small tin shed that served as his office and home. It had no air-conditioning and only a small electric heater. He slept on a cot in the corner. The cars were rusty, most were missing parts, and some had been wrecked. Actually it wasn't a museum at all; it was a junkyard. He gave Mark a bottle of moonshine as a college graduation gift.

Mark had partial scholarship offers from Vanderbilt and Sewanee, but he chose to stay in Poplar Grove to look after his mother. He finished first in his class at Pearl River College and started his job managing the grocery store the Monday after college graduation. He paid rent for his own apartment and paid his mother's house note. He also helped with his mother's medical expenses and her utility bills. Although he never complained, it was impossible for Mark to save anything for university enrollment.

"I never consider taking care of my mother a burden. Wish I could do more."

He worked part time as a bank teller and grocery delivery boy, and cut grass on weekends. He finished the associate degree one semester early because he took extra summer classes. Clarence complimented Mark and said he was a "go-getter." Mark admired and respected Clarence as well.

"Thank you for teaching me. I want to sell a lot of cars." Mark was excited about the amount of money he expected to make at his new career.

Right away Clarence noticed an attraction between Mark and Melissa. He encouraged things by getting them together as much as possible. He asked Melissa to help teach Mark the business side of selling. She explained the paperwork process and warranty details.

"No deal is done until the paperwork is complete," she said.

Clarence also asked her to introduce Mark around the dealership and show him the best restaurants for lunch. Melissa looked in Clarence's direction, raised the corner of her right eyebrow, and gave him the most beautiful smile. She knew what he was up to. Mark and Melissa went to lunch together every day for two weeks. Clarence enjoyed watching the young romance blossom.

Melissa's husband was back in rehab after he was arrested in another bar fight. The judge gave him a choice between jail or rehab. She had enough and finally ended the marriage. "I can't do this anymore!" she said while her husband pleaded for one more chance.

"But I love you, baby! Please don't do this." He was on his knees. "Where am I supposed to go?"

Somehow, she found the courage to kick him out for good. Clarence cared about Melissa a great deal and wanted her to find happiness.

Mark learned sales by watching Clarence close deals. "Persuasion is not an art; it is a science." Clarence explained the steps to a successful sales career. He introduced Mark to customers and asked for their help training him. "Do you mind if Mark observes our negotiations?" No one objected and most were happy to help. Clarence and Mark sold numerous big Lincolns, Fords, and inexpensive used cars. They treated all customers with respect and dignity. Mark learned that every customer is important and every sale worthwhile.

Clarence spent as much time with an 800-dollar used-car shopper as the buyer of a new Lincoln Continental. "The poor man's eight hundred dollars is just as important to him as another man's thirty thousand. Besides, you never know how things can go. That same customer may show up next year to buy a new Lincoln," he taught Mark.

Spencer never objected to Clarence's sense of fair play because he sold so many cars. Spencer was stupid but not dumb enough to fire a gifted salesman.

Mark learned how to give customers a good deal and make a living for himself as well. "Treat customers fair, you will sleep well, and you won't need to constantly look over your shoulder. It does no one any good if the repo man shows up," Clarence said. He never offered extended warrantees because they were ridiculously expensive, and he never sold dealer-added undercoating.

"If a new car needs dealer-applied undercoating to stop rust, then it is junk anyway," Clarence believed.

Clarence wouldn't call the "manager" even if he was having trouble closing a valuable sale. Spencer was sure to screw the customers, and Clarence kept him far away. "If I can't close the deal in a fair manner, then it just can't be done. Besides, customers do not want to be jerked around like that," Clarence explained.

Mark learned how interest rates and trade-in allowances affected the final price. "Most salesmen will reduce the new car price if necessary to close the deal but get the money back by offering a low trade allowance and charging high interest rates. Don't do that. We don't need to trick anybody." All the other salesmen were told that Mark trained only with Clarence. He wanted to protect Mark from the dishonest misadventure Spencer encouraged.

"This is the best purchase experience ever. It could serve as a customer model for others who do business with the public. I can't imagine any sales group doing it better," a happy customer said.

Mark took the buyer around his new car, pointing out everything he needed to know. Mark was unhurried and professional. They all shook hands and the customer drove away happy in his new Lincoln.

Clarence established the "C and M" sales team, naming Mark his junior partner, which allowed them to share commissions while avoiding Spencer's rip-off scams. Melissa shredded the original contract and placed the new document in Mark's employment file. Surprisingly, Robert said nothing. Lately, he was spending all his time searching ads for classic Thunderbird convertibles and talking about the Florida Keys.

"I haven't taken a vacation since the Carter administration. I'm not getting any younger," he said, ignoring Clarence's questions about Mark's commission payout rate. "Do what you want." A week later Robert's desk was cleaned out and his personal items removed. He left a short note. "Too many years wasted. Too much time forgotten."

It is an amazing thing, the power of words. For decades Robert loved his management role and enjoyed helping build the dealership. He met Mark and now he was driving to the Florida Keys in a sixty-year-old automobile. Only certain people have this valuable gift. They influence behavior using words to motivate new thinking. History remembers Martin Luther King, Lincoln, and Ronald Reagan. Mark had this gift. He could become a remarkable lawyer, accomplishing significant achievements. Andre told Clarence Mark should be studying at Tulane.

"Okay, Andre, I'll start sprinkling the Tulane dust on him every day," Clarence said. He enjoyed encouraging friends.

George Graves became concerned. After many calls all week long, he had been unable to reach Spencer or Robert. Melissa had been instructed to give out no information to anyone.

"They are temporarily unavailable. I have no additional information at this time," she said repeatedly as instructed.

On Sunday afternoons when the dealership was closed, Spencer allowed George to use the mechanic shop to work on his 1976 El Camino. Spencer said George was "bad for business," so he was allowed to visit only when the dealership was closed. But George was worried, so he stopped by the showroom on Thursday afternoon looking for Spencer and Robert.

"I haven't been able to reach anyone for days. What's going on? Spencer! Spencer! Robert!" George called out. He was loud and caused everyone to look in his direction.

"Everything is fine, George. I'll have Spencer call you tomorrow. Now run along," Melissa tried to reassure him while showing him the door.

As a drugstore delivery boy, Mark had been to George's home many times. "That's a strange guy," Mark said to Clarence, explaining his many weird encounters with George. "Once, I delivered a prescription and a case of Cokes to his home. No one answered the front door, so I walked around back. I saw George lying flat on his back under the chicken coop. He said he had never actually seen a chicken lay an egg before. But the strangest thing of all is the tooth he keeps in a jar on a shelf. He sure is proud of that tooth. Very creepy."

Clarence agreed with Mark. "I remember seeing that tooth as well. It was the day before my lawn party. I knocked on his front door to invite him. George seems to have all his natural front teeth. Why would he want to keep someone else's?"

The Statute of Limitations is designed to prevent claims and charges from arising after all evidence has been lost to time. Facts become obscured, witnesses die or disappear, and memories become cloudy with the passing years. But the statute does not apply to murder. "I do not think anyone would be stupid enough to keep incriminating hate crime evidence, like a lynched victim's tooth, displayed on a shelf in their home." Andre was skeptical and told Clarence so. He reminded Andre that George was very dumb.

"This is the same guy who told everyone in town his roosters lay eggs. George is the guy who got stuck in my backyard well. He is the same guy who does not know the difference between Tabasco and tobacco or how to spell 'trespassing.' He thinks hamburgers and steaks are different if purchased at a black-owned business, and he killed my cats!"

Andre agreed with Clarence. Maybe George could actually be that stupid.

23

NEWS OF RUSSELL'S DEATH SPREAD throughout every nook and cranny of the Louisiana political grapevine like Formosan termites swarming on a summer night. It did not take long before the political rats began leaving Russell's sinking empire. The Louisiana Secretary of Health and Hospitals was the first to say he was shocked to learn of the abuses taking place in Russell's nursing homes.

Federal investigations led to numerous front-page stories. In response, the Louisiana Secretary of Health and Hospitals called a news conference to explain what the state was doing to "protect our most vulnerable citizens during this difficult time. We had no idea…" He assured everyone that his office would get to the bottom of this.

"We are shocked at the abuse and neglect that have gone undetected for too long! However, after internal reviews, we believe with confidence that Mr. Russell Burley orchestrated all of this independent of any state knowledge or public employee or elected official involvement of any kind."

But some of Russell's former associates and employees volunteered testimony to FBI investigators. The first person to squeal usually gets the best deal. Everyone else gets indicted and goes to jail. It becomes a race to see who can get to the grand jury first, either to save their own skin or throw others under the bus.

"Russell cheated everyone, even when it was not necessary. He screwed me and everyone associated with educational products." The drunken college professor from UNO provided names of politicians involved with the sale and promotion of Russell's remedial math DVDs.

"I asked Russell for supplies. He refused my requests. I did the best I could with the resources I had. We could not buy toilet paper, repair TVs, or fix air conditioners, but I always had envelopes full of hundred-dollar bills on hand for the health inspectors." Saint Ann's head nurse provided the grand jury with names of corrupt government auditors and inspectors. "Everyone got an envelope. Russell said we don't need to worry about state license visits and inspections because everyone is on his payroll." She testified that Saint Ann's always received exceptional reviews and high health department scores.

"Russell planned to open a group home in a middle-class area near Abita Springs. The community organized against it with twelve different neighborhood groups working together in opposition," the nurse testified.

Russell took Saint Ann's head nurse with him to the approval hearing to help answer questions. "Two hundred people signed up to speak against us. But Russell was not worried. He said everyone on the council got an envelope. Russell sat in the back of the council chambers reading *Sports Illustrated*. The motion to approve Russell's new group home eventually carried unanimously," she said.

"These homes are highly profitable enterprises. What do I care if I give some nickel-dick politician ten thousand dollars? It is just a cost of doing business, but then I own them. I like pet humans." The nurse said Russell bragged about having politicians in his back pocket.

She said she never liked Russell but needed the job. "His penis was like a raw oyster. It was cold, soft, and slimy. He needed Viagra. He was also very strange. I fell asleep at his house after hours of heavy drinking. During the night he shaved my pussy. I had a hell of a time explaining that to my husband." The district attorney instructed the grand jury members to disregard comments about Russell's penis and sexual deviations.

The governor claimed he had always been suspicious of Russell. "I never trusted him. Something about that man wasn't right."

He insisted that the full power and resources of the state would be directed toward taking care of the nursing home residents Russell neglected. "State agencies are working closely with federal authorities to figure out how these inadequate facilities were allowed to operate for so long." The governor expressed shock that it was all done for money. He said Russell was a very rich man. "Now we all know how he got his wealth."

Skeptical of the governor's public statements, Andre filed individual lawsuits on behalf of Mr. Richard and Mr. Gains, claiming neglect and abuse at Saint Ann's. This gave them legal standing as participating parties. Andre also joined as a "Friend of the Court" in all proceedings involving the other nursing homes. He was concerned that the court's decisions should not depend solely on political skullduggery and deal making but on broad concerns of deep-rooted corruption involving the alleged sale of nursing homes and hospital operating licenses. Andre had always been suspicious of Louisiana politicians, and he suspected bribery, extortion, and racketeering reaching the highest levels of Louisiana state government.

His amicus brief questioned the unlikely possibility that all this was done by Russell without the help of both low-level bureaucrats and high-ranking Louisiana politicians, including the governor. Russell was operating a racket. Andre believed the alleged crimes fit the Racketeer Influenced and Corrupt Organizations Act. "The FBI will consider Russell's enterprises and business practices as a RICO matter. It is only a matter of time before other coconspirators and persons of interest are named." Andre's prediction generated angry responses claiming irresponsible statements would damage the careers of trusted public servants.

"Hungry lawyers and other charlatans will use this unfortunate situation to make money. Don't listen to them. They are snake oil salesmen just like Russell." The governor tried to deflect criticism by attacking and discrediting his accusers, especially Andre!

Most politicians are too clever to simply accept cash kickbacks. Real corruption scams are sophisticated and involve layers of protection hiding payment sources and receipts. But there are always exceptions to every rule. A state representative built a 5,000-square-foot home with indoor pool and basketball court. He earned about forty-five thousand dollars annually from his state salary and pro-diem expenses.

"I know how to manage money," he told investigators before his sentencing hearing.

Innumerable legends about "blank checks" were important in the fantastic stories about Louisiana political corruption. The checks were a metaphor for political kickbacks. Enterprising governors won homes and Italian sports cars in card games, their wives made fortunes workings as consultants or lobbyists, and others hid real-estate interest disguised behind corporate veils. Governor Earl Long called all of this "honest graft." Andre was determined to figure out how the Louisiana governor was rewarded for quarterbacking the nursing home license racket. Always follow the money.

Many Louisiana corruption stories, like the "deduct box," were just intrigue and legend that had been enriched over the years. The deduct box was where Governor Huey Long allegedly hid the money he extorted from the paychecks of state workers. It was never found.

"Huey, where's the deduct box? Where's the box?" Earl Long asked after Huey was shot.

But Huey died before revealing its location. Although the actual box was never discovered, the Long family always had the where-withal to run political campaigns. Huey left a political blank check that his descendants had cashed for generations.

A few Louisiana blank-check stories were based on actual fact. Victor Schiro was elected councilman at-large before becoming mayor of

New Orleans. As councilman at-large he served as mayor pro tem anytime the real mayor was out of town.

Victor Schiro was sitting at the mayor's desk, as he often did, when his phone rang. Two Germans came to see him. They were executives with an unfamiliar foreign car company seeking a Louisiana distributor. "We need someone politically connected with a strong understanding of the South Louisiana market and a background of proven success in automobile distribution and brand marketing."

Schiro thought the Germans were wasting their money.

"Americans won't buy a tiny foreign car designed for Hitler." The mayor pro tem suggested they would have better success concentrating sales efforts in Italy and Spain. "Americans love their Detroit Lincoln, Imperial, and Cadillac. We are patriotic and don't favor foreign cars with strange names. That will never change." No one ever accused Victor Schiro of being smart. After Hurricane Betsy flooded the city, he told citizens, "Don't believe any false rumors unless you hear them from me first!"

Victor introduced the Germans to "Honest Ron, The Walking Man's Pal" his friend who owned three small used-car lots located around the city. His advertising slogan claimed his business was just about right: "Large enough to satisfy, small enough to work hard at it."

With Victor's encouragement the Germans gave Honest Ron the Volkswagen distribution rights for all of South Louisiana. He made a percentage on every Beatle the Germans sold for the next twenty-five years. Thereafter anytime Victor ran a new political campaign, he could count on receiving a blank check from Honest Ron. "Fill in any amount you need." The modern Louisiana political campaign contribution and spending limit laws were enacted because of Victor Schiro and Honest Ron.

Unlimited resources can be provided to punish a political rival and to exact revenge as well. Andre was back in New Orleans at his desk the next week. A letter from Mr. Pavel Navalny, addressed to "My

Friend," was waiting. He requested wire transfer instructions for Andre's law firm's bank accounts. "There is no limit to what I will spend. Andre, continue doing whatever it takes. Destroy their careers, personal lives, and fortunes. Strip them of everything. I want them begging on their knees. I want these men praying for death over the few miserable crumbs of dignity their lives will have left."

Mr. Navalny's letter included suggestions for legal strategies and ways he planned to finish off John's grocery business. He left Spencer to Andre. His blank check was for the prosecution, conviction, and personal destruction of the men who hurt Alexi. He especially wanted the governor's scalp.

"I am not a killer. I am a good father," he reminded Andre.

24

FROM TIME TO TIME LOCAL car dealers need to pick up vehicles from out-of-town dealerships when a customer has a request for an unusual and hard-to-find model or color. The only available two-tone blue Lincoln Town Car sedan in the area was located at a dealership in uptown New Orleans on Saint Charles Avenue. Lesley promised delivery in a few days. The customer was eager and a cash buyer, but he did not mind a short delay. Early Wednesday morning two employees would drive to New Orleans together in a service vehicle and pick up the new Lincoln. They would return that afternoon with both cars. Meals and expenses were placed on a company credit card. Lesley called Mark and Melissa into the office.

"On second thought, New Orleans is a long drive and we do have five days until delivery." For safety reasons Lesley changed company policy and required two nights' rest in a New Orleans hotel. "Driving while drowsy is extremely dangerous," she explained. Lesley was a romantic like Clarence, and she adored Mark and Melissa. Clarence assured Mark that he could handle sales on his own for three days.

"I know you have the company credit card, but take this. Have some fun." Clarence placed five one-hundred-dollar bills in Mark's shirt pocket. Melissa spent a weekend in Biloxi when she was six years old. The family stayed at the old Holiday Inn on the bay. She remembered the swimming pool and the color TV in the room. It was the only vacation she ever had.

New Orleans police worked hard to keep tourist areas safe, especially in the French Quarter, uptown, and along the streetcar lines. Melissa said she had never been to uptown New Orleans. She had never ridden a streetcar during a summer rain, walked Tulane's campus, or picnicked in Audubon Park with a new lover. She never enjoyed a cup of morning coffee at a sidewalk café on Magazine Street while listening to WWOZ, a great non-profit jazz station. Melissa hadn't spent a Saturday afternoon sitting on the Mississippi River levee counting passing tugs and barges. The river's flow to the gulf was eternal, yet the view was always changing.

Hotel Lafayette was located on Saint Charles Avenue, a few miles from Tulane University. It was close to Canal Street; streetcars passed directly in front. The location was convenient, next to Lafayette Square. The park was designed in 1788 and had statues of Ben Franklin and Henry Clay. The old New Orleans City Hall faced the park on the north side of Saint Charles Avenue. The hotel was a few steps away.

In 1869, the Louisiana legislature legalized gambling in New Orleans. From Lafayette Square to Canal Street, there were forty gambling halls and bordellos. They never closed their doors, and locals referred to them as the "forty thieves" because most of the games, like faro, roulette, and keno, were crooked. The establishments sold homemade Irish whisky and brandy. They made the whisky by dumping creosote into a barrel of moonshine.

They created homemade brandy by "mixing a barrel of moonshine with water. Then we added prune juice, two pounds of burnt sugar, and olive oil. Sulfuric acid and chewing tobacco gave the mixture sparkle. I made a five percent commission on all alcohol sales," a bartender admitted after four patrons died during a night of heavy drinking.

Today, free lunchtime jazz concerts on weekdays and food booths offering local Creole and Cajun seafood specialties draw large crowds of locals and tourists to the area.

Streetcars make a clacking sound as they rumble down ancient tracks, electrical connections spark and pop, and conductors ring a bell at each intersection. They call out the names of each approaching stop, "Napoleon Avenue, Jackson Avenue, Washington Avenue."

Daydreaming passengers sit lost in lonely thoughts. Side by side, lovers hug as young lovers do. Their anticipation grows steamy as city streets, live oaks, and grand Victorian homes roll past the open windows. The sounds of trumpets drift faintly in the air from nearby jazz clubs. Every New Orleans streetcar could be named Desire. It is hard not to fall in love in this romantic part of the city. A hotel room on the Saint Charles Avenue streetcar line is to romance what honey is to bees or trumpets to jazz. A little taste encourages a desire for more.

Mark said he and Melissa planned to "check into our room, have a quick lunch in Lafayette Square, then ride the streetcar to the Lincoln dealership, making sure everything is squared away."

The hotel's magnificent lobby was decorated with crystal chandeliers hanging from towering ceilings and walls of paneling and wood inlays. Renaissance paintings decorated the walls. A marble stairway led to a second-floor restaurant and balcony. Mark approached the registration desk and presented his confirmation number, expecting a small room with two double beds. "Sir, please wait one moment." The clerk left and returned with the hotel manager.

"Your reservations have been upgraded. May I show you to our Bienville suite? It is the finest available. Your friends are generous and care about you very much."

The manager was dressed in a seersucker blue striped suit with white and tan oxford shoes. He personally escorted Mark and Melissa to the hotel's top floor and handed them a card with a short handwritten note from Lesley and Clarence.

"Life is full of wonderful and unexpected turns. Enjoy New Orleans." It was signed in blue ink.

Lesley took a call from Alexi. They were becoming close and talked often. Alexi was doing much better now and talked about happy things. "I am so excited about college." She asked Lesley about college boys. That fall she would enroll as a freshman at Yale. She had not decided on a major but had many interests. She invited Lesley to help her move into the dorm room.

"Of course, I would love to." Lesley suggested they first go on a dorm-furnishing shopping spree.

Lesley sat behind Spencer's desk and began going through files. Clarence was in a chair to the right. She called Mr. Washington first. "The dealership has run a special contest for our best customers. You are a winner. If you can visit the dealership tomorrow, our service department will install four brand-new radial tires on your truck. There will be absolutely no charge to you!" Mr. Washington was the old farmer Spencer cheated by selling him his own used tires back.

"I ain't never won nothin'. You sure you have the right Mr. Washington?"

Lesley assured him this was not a trick.

Janine said she missed her husband terribly but could not trust her car to make the trip to Houston. The cost of rebuilding the cooling system set her back six months, and now the transmission was failing. She did not have any money, and the children needed many things. Her husband worked two jobs in Houston and sent back as much cash as he could. "He shares a one-bedroom apartment with four other construction workers. He eats potted meat sandwiches for lunch every day. He sends us every penny he can," Janine said.

"It seems some parts we installed on your car may have been defective. That may be the reason your transmission is failing. We want to make this right," Lesley explained.

"I don't have any money, and I can't spend another penny on that old car. It should be in a junkyard, but I can't afford another. I appreciate the call." Janine was about to hang up.

"The transmission is failing because the car is still overheating. This is our fault. I want you to bring your car to the dealership tomorrow. We have a nice minivan that is perfect for your young family and perfect for many comfortable and safe trips to Houston. Even trade, you owe us nothing. We want satisfied customers." Lesley worked hard to convince Janine this was not a trick or joke of some kind.

Lesley spent all afternoon making similar calls like this. Her final call was placed to Andre's law firm. They began drawing up divorce papers. She reached out her hand to Clarence. They embraced. Clarence used his index finger to wipe away her tears.

"I'm not crying about the divorce. I'm sad about wasting so many years." Lesley refused Clarence's dinner offer and instead she unbuttoned his shirt.

She enjoyed caressing his powerful chest. The arousing pulse of his heart felt reassuring against her bare breasts. She swept the top of Spencer's desk clean with her left arm. His Wildcat football helmet rolled across the office floor. Doing it on top of Spencer's desk was very erotic.

"Looking for a roommate?" Lesley asked.

Mark walked across the hotel room and opened the windows. "I rode the streetcar once, when I was about seven. My dad was here for a job interview. He didn't want the potential new employer to see his beat-up Oldsmobile, so we parked a few blocks away and rode the streetcar to the job interview. Back then my parents were still in love. They sat side by side holding hands." Melissa wanted Mark to relax and unwind. He agreed that the room was remarkable.

"Let's ride the streetcar later today. I want to hear about your parents," she said.

Melissa then spun around in circles with her arms outstretched. Her white cotton dress lifted up ever so slightly. She reminded Mark of Julie Andrews in the opening scene of *The Sound of Music*.

"I have never seen a room like this. It's so beautiful. I can't believe we are here!" She became dizzy and fell flat on her back on top of the king-sized bed.

Outside, a streetcar conductor called out the next stop, "Girod Street." The car rumbled on down the tracks. Sounds of a jazz band performing in the square drifted into the room through the open windows. "Do you know what it means to miss New Orleans and miss it each night and day?" Singing about the lazy Mississippi and moonlight on the bayou, the singer sounded like Fats Domino. Melissa held out her hand for Mark and pulled him toward her.

Melissa told Lesley Mark was very shy at first. "I realized he was unlikely to make the first move. I unhooked my bra from the back and guided Mark's hand, placing it under my dress. I tossed the bra to the floor and unbuttoned his shirt." Lesley was surprised how uninhibited the younger generation was about discussing these things.

The open windows brought the New Orleans summer heat and humidity inside the room. The sweltering temperature provided a good excuse to remove the rest of their clothes.

"I sat up and pulled my dress over my head."

Melissa unzipped Mark's pants and playfully used her feet to push them down past his knees. Their sweaty bodies moved together. Another streetcar passed by. Mark rested for a few minutes then they loved each other again.

"Something magical about this old city," Melissa admitted.

A hotel employee quietly slipped an envelope under the hotel room door. It was a letter from Andre's dear friend, Dr. Phillip Reck, Dean of Tulane's College of Continuing Education. He was always looking for smart students and prided himself on recruiting bright students from unlikely places. Andre suggested he should meet Mark.

25

THE IDEA MOST PEOPLE HAVE of the legal profession is learned from watching late night commercials starring ambulance chasers promising big checks.

"Call today, get your check tomorrow. I will personally return your call." They guarantee anything.

Attorneys have a well-earned representation for being snakes. Most likely everyone knows a good lawyer joke. "What does a lawyer get when you give him Viagra? Taller." Or, "Why do lawyers always wear ties? It keeps the foreskin from coming up over their heads."

However, on a serious note, well-trained lawyers also have the opportunity to use the legal system to defend and protect the weak and feeble. It is amazing how effective a threatening, well-written legal letter is.

Since Mr. Gains was no longer imprisoned at Saint Ann's, getting his property back was a relatively simple legal exercise.

Andre sent letters to the prospective new buyers of his home, the closing real-estate agent and company, Mr. Gains' family, and the County Register of Conveyances. He explained multiple serious, unresolved title issues since Mr. Gains owned the property and intended to move back in immediately.

"Any sale of this property is illegal since my client is not selling his home." Andre included title search and county tax records showing Mr. Gains as owner of his home for decades. The exasperated buyers quickly moved on to consider other less encumbered properties. The sale was canceled.

Andre would seldom use threats of criminal charges to settle a civil matter, but Mr. Gains' family should have been charged with elder abuse and theft. They insisted that everything they did was for the benefit of Mr. Gains. "We love our uncle and were only trying to help him." Andre was not convinced and suggested a conversation with the district attorney. They willingly agreed to return everything they had taken and refund all proceeds obtained at the fraudulent estate sale.

Many of Mr. Gains' larger antique furniture pieces were purchased by an antique auction house in Hattiesburg called Neil Cody's Estate Auctions. It had been a successful and trusted business at the same downtown location for thirty-five years. The Latin motto "Dictum meum pactum," which means, "My word is my bond," was printed on the delivery trucks and business cards. Mr. Cody was a good business person and would not risk anything that could damage his reputation. All items were returned to Poplar Grove the very next day and placed in Mr. Gains' home as promised. Neil Cody filed a suit against Mr. Gains' family seeking to recover his losses and expenses. Under the circumstances his full recovery would be a simple open-and-shut legal matter.

Richard was helping Mr. Gains move back into his house when he received a call that changed his life. It seemed Pavel Navalny needed a Director of Governmental Operations. The position included protecting and defending the company's interest before US agencies, Congress, foreign governments, and extensive international travel. Richard would also author position papers supporting energy development around the world. It was a lucrative position that reported directly to Pavel Navalny, with an office on the top floor of the international headquarters building in Houston.

"I have many enemies and a reputation as a troublemaker. Much of my best work has been discredited, and I am out of the loop on the most important current issues. My health has not been very good." Richard was afraid that he was wrong for the job and did not want to disappoint Mr. Navalny. He had no self-confidence left. "I appreciate the offer but I cannot accept," he said politely and offered to refer someone else.

"We all have enemies and I also have a reputation as a trouble-maker. We will get along fine." Pavel offered to move Richard to Houston next week.

It did not take long before word got around that Richard was going to work for Pavel Navalny. *Foreign Affairs* magazine ran an article about the triumphant return of Richard Tower. Old enemies and old friends all called. His wife was one of the first.

"Congratulations on your new job. I'm so proud and still love you and miss you so much." She asked to see Richard again. "I don't remember what went wrong between us," she said.

She lived in horrible conditions. Her singlewide trailer had no air-conditioning, and the carpets had been ruined by cats because she was too lazy or disinterested to change the litter box. The windows were covered with old newspapers. She had repaired broken glass on the front door with cardboard from a cigarette carton. Her lover left long ago and she lived alone with bad teeth, diabetes, and cats. She had a gambling problem and spent hours each day playing slot machines at Biloxi casinos, wasting the monthly income she swindled from Richard. It was all very sad.

She asked to borrow two hundred dollars. "Just to get me through till next month," she explained. Surprisingly, Richard did not feel satisfaction or vindication; he just felt indifferent. He handed her all the cash in his wallet, about seventy-five dollars.

"You're still a cheap, no-good bastard," she said.

Richard headed to the airport, where a private jet was waiting. He did not look back.

26

THE SAINT CHARLES STREETCAR STOPPED directly in front of Tulane's Gibson Hall across from Audubon Park. The historic sandstone building was used for administration purposes, including undergrad admissions, the president's office, and the School of Continuing Education. Dr. Reck was waiting in his first-floor office when Mark and Melissa walked over from the streetcar stop. He was eager to meet Mark and had arranged a campus tour and a visit to the Law School.

"Tulane University is not cheap, nor should it be." Mark read the first few pages of a Tulane recruiting brochure. "How much is Tulane's reputation as one of the world's leading universities worth? A lot!" Mark put the pamphlet down. He pulled Melissa toward him and whispered, "I don't belong at a school like this. Let's get out of here." He explained to Dr. Reck that Tulane was way out of his price range.

"I don't have this kind of money now and am not likely to in the future. Sorry to have wasted your time." Mark was apologetic and polite.

Melissa had never seen Mark so disappointed and defeated. "We have come this far and don't have anything else planned today." She held both his hands, looked into his eyes, encouraging him to stay. "Why not? You have nothing to lose. Let's see what they have to say." She was reassuring.

"Tulane is expensive, yes, and extremely challenging as well. But a degree from Tulane University represents a world-class education. You will learn to think beyond yourself, recognizing and appreciating the wonders of art, history, languages, and philosophy as well as law." Dr. Reck was pleased Mark decided to stay for the tour. "Most likely the decision will represent a significant turning point in your life." Dr. Reck slid a thick, dark green folder across the table toward Mark. "Please open it," he suggested.

Melissa felt Mark's pulse race as he carefully opened the folder and saw a Tulane degree up close. It was like holding a Fabergé egg, captivating and priceless. "Have you ever seen anything more remarkable?" Mark asked Melissa. He ran his fingers across the heavily engraved print.

"I know you can do this. I can see your name printed here." Melissa pointed to the first line on the degree.

The Tulane College of Continuing Education had been around for decades; it was previously called University College. The college was designed to provide a Tulane education to nontraditional students. Single parents and working people seeking career advancement or exploring academic passions took conveniently scheduled evening and weekend classes with agreeable tuition rates. The professors were the same who taught traditional Tulane classes, and the academic expectations and standards were not compromised. However, the admissions process was streamlined to accommodate busy schedules, and academic credits from state universities and community colleges were accepted for transfer in lieu of some regular admission requirements. Tulane's College of Continuing Education was perfect for a student like Mark.

As Dr. Reck began the campus tour, he explained scholarship opportunities and the Law School admission process available upon the successful completion of the undergrad degree program. "Nearly all incoming students receive some level of financial aid. Also you will meet other students from Europe, Asia, South and Central America, and all fifty states. Moreover, ninety percent of prelaw students are accepted into the law school of their choice. But many undergrads decide to study law at Tulane."

They walked past Hebert Hall and the Richardson Building. Melissa loved the live oaks and manicured lawns. They crossed Freret Street and entered McAlister Place. The Law School building was on the right. Prelaw curriculum included the humanities, social science, philosophy, political science, and history. They continued walking.

"Most prelaw students take their liberal arts classes in that building." Dr. Reck pointed to Newcomb Hall. "Last year the average Tulane LSAT score was 162."

He explained that every accredited Law School required a certain score on the Law School Admissions Test. "It is like the ACT for law schools," he said.

"Many New Orleans law firms offer scholarship opportunities for Tulane students. Louisiana is the only state with a legal system based upon the Napoleonic Code, not British Common Law. This uniqueness makes it difficult for New Orleans firms to hire lawyers from the other forty-nine states. Nearly forty percent of Tulane Law School grads find employment in Louisiana. Don't worry about the money. Worry about the opportunity you lose if you don't even try." Dr. Reck convinced Mark to complete the admission applications and take a chance.

"Success and happiness cannot exist without some risk," he said.

Melissa and Mark decided to have lunch at the famous Camellia Grill on Carrollton and Saint Charles Avenue. They sat at the lunch counter on 1940s-style art deco chrome stools. Mark ordered a cheeseburger and onion rings.

"Dressed with mynez?" the waiter asked.

Melissa ordered the Camellia Club sandwich and Coke. The friendly waiter joked about her Mississippi accent and promised to teach her "how ta tawk right."

"Really! Your New Orleans accent is so heavy I don't know what you're saying. Is that even English?" she playfully asked.

New Orleans is a southern city, but locals didn't speak with a typical southern drawl; it is more of a Brooklyn-ese style with a strong French influence. This is most common with those from Chalmette and Ninth Ward areas of the city.

"It don' madda," he said. The waiter liked Melissa's "gumption" and presented her with a certificate naming her an Honorary Camellia Grill Boogalee. He explained that a Boogalee was a good-looking and smart Cajun. Other waiters gathered around and clapped, recognizing Melissa's award the way other restaurants acknowledge birthdays. She blushed and promised to frame her new credential.

"I may even add it to my resume," she jested.

The coffee and chicory was on the house. Chicory is a roasted root that locals add to already very strong coffee, giving it more kick and flavor. Melissa absolutely loved it and asked for a refill. It was too strong for Mark.

"My god, that's potent! What the heck!" He looked down at his spoon, surprised it was not eaten away as if by acid. He asked for a glass of water.

The waiter taught Mark to say "soc au lait" instead of "what the heck."

"People in Naw'lins don' say things like dat," he explained.

Holding hands, Mark and Melissa headed back to the streetcar. All the waiters waved good-bye.

27

LESLEY WOKE FIRST AND GENTLY kissed Clarence's forehead, careful not to wake him. She loved reading the morning paper at sunup. Clarence's backyard was beautiful this early time of day, with dew on the grass and sunbeams reflecting off the pool's surface. The summer morning was surprisingly cool and damp. Lesley wrapped herself in a knit blanket and snuggled warmly on the back porch swing. Clarence woke later. He poured two bowls of cornflakes and sliced a fresh cantaloupe. He made a pot of fresh coffee and brought Lesley a cup. She liked two percent milk and artificial sweetener. They enjoyed breakfast together.

"I'm happy," she said.

Lesley had been reading a front-page article about the unfortunate hot tub death of Russell Burley and the size of his estate.

"It says that much of his wealth is wrapped up in a limited liability corporation called American Community Care Centers. I know that name. It rings a bell but I can't place it." She didn't think much more about it then, but she knew it would bug her until she remembered.

Lesley wrote the corporate name down, planning to research it later when she returned to her office that afternoon. Clarence sat next to her on the swing, and they finished reading the paper together.

"Fraudulent corporations often use impressive words like International, American, European, or Atlantic in their title to convey a false impression of stature and importance. They deliberately craft corporate names to mislead, creating a false sense of legitimacy," Lesley said, still bugged by the newspaper article.

Like a light bulb, she suddenly remembered where she had first seen the name American Community Care Centers before.

"That's it! This is the corporation that first purchased the Louisiana governor's Poplar Grove property. They originally purchased it for corporate management, training, and retreat purposes. We were all so excited about the influx of well-paid professionals spending money in Poplar Grove. Surprisingly American Community Care Centers sold the estate a very short while later, claiming it was unsuitable for their unique needs. As a cash buyer the governor got quite a bargain, and the corporation benefited from an immense tax write-off for the extensive real-estate loss."

"That seems like a very convenient coincidence. Especially if the corporation was owned by Russell and the property was sold to the governor at a bargain basement price." Clarence asked Lesley if this could be some type of sophisticated money-laundering and kickback scheme.

"Bogus corporations often try to exchange inflated assets for stock in a legitimate company. They then create fake financial statements based on the value of the inflated assets and the newly acquired legitimate stock. They use the overvalued statements to solicit other investors. The legitimate assets are then sold off or used as collateral securing bank loans. The loans are never paid back. It is a common money-laundering scam." Lesley also said that in this case the incentive would be political corruption and kickbacks, not simple bank fraud.

Clarence went back into the kitchen for more coffee.

"This reminds me of a childhood acquaintance," he said. "Leonora came from a large Italian family with four brothers and three sisters.

They were very wealthy and lived in an expensive home on the lakefront with servants and gardeners. The children went to the best private schools and drove expensive cars.

"Every Sunday the family hosted large family dinners. Leonora's mother was a wonderful cook and loved to prepare traditional Italian dishes. She cooked ravioli, chicken parmesan, lasagna, spaghetti with baked meatballs, and Italian sausage. Everything was served family style on trays and platters placed in the center of the table and shared unselfishly. Colorful conversation flowed back and forth. The brothers spoke Sicilian with gusto. The grand finale was the generous servings of Leonora's homemade tiramisu. I was invited once and was surprised when Carlos Marcello arrived," Clarence said.

"Carlos Marcello the mob boss? The guy implicated in the Kennedy assassination?" Lesley asked.

"Yes. But Mr. Marcello always said he was just a poor tomato farmer, and Leonora's family always said they owned only one business, the Lakeview Snowball stand on Harrison Avenue and Argonne Street." Clarence asked Lesley if the snowball business could have been a front used to pay mob kickbacks and launder illegal money, similar to what Russell was doing.

"I always wondered how selling snowballs could be so profitable," Clarence said.

"Sounds like the same basic operation with one exception. Leonora's family was most likely running a front business to launder money for organized crime; Russell was a rainmaker for corrupt politicians. Very similar but different," Lesley said.

"The mob ran cash earned from their lawless operations through the snowball business, paying taxes on every penny of fake profits, thus legalizing the cash. It is a great idea. Who is going to suspect a neighborhood snowball stand as a mob front business? What bothers me most about Russell's scam is the fact that taxpayers got the bill."

"Russell's corporation sold a two-million-dollar property for one hundred and fifty thousand dollars to the governor. The Louisiana governor got rich while taxpayers covered the cost of American Community Care Center's corporate loss write-off. On paper it looked like the governor was a shrewd real-estate investor, not a crooked politician taking kickbacks from selling nursing home licenses. It's all very clever!" Lesley said.

"Should the FBI know about this?" Clarence wondered.

The Bureau was always interested in investigating political corruption, but they also started a Cold Case Initiative seeking to solve open Civil Rights-era hate crimes. Of 124 suspected race crimes, three dozen murders were now reopened, active investigations, including the 1959 killing of Mack Parker in Poplar Grove.

The special agent in charge was happy to take Andre's call.

"Andre, we are seeking cases that can still be prosecuted. Age and infirmity offer no refuge for those guilty of these lynchings. However, time is our greatest challenge at this late date; witnesses are dying off, and evidence has disappeared with time," the FBI agent said over the phone. They discussed the information Andre had and also the possibility of undiscovered physical evidence of the crime still existing in Poplar Grove.

The old days when the FBI worked to cover up hate crimes had long since passed. Early the next morning three agents were in Andre's office. They flew overnight from Washington, DC in a Bureau jet, landing at the New Orleans Lakefront Airport. Eager to meet, they skipped breakfast. Andre discussed everything he knew about Mr. Gains' story. They were especially interested in his theory about the circumstances surrounding George Graves's birth. The agents already knew many details of Mack's murder but were able to fill in some additional holes with this new information. Later that same day they planned to meet with Mr. Gains.

"This all seems to fit together. Do you have any idea which individual was called Scalper? That name comes up often." The agents also asked more questions about George Graves.

"During our first conversation you also mentioned something about the possibility of significant new evidence. This is most important!" All the agents were taking notes. The lead agent said the FBI had located and contacted many surviving family members of hate crime victims in efforts to provide them with information on the reopened cases.

"We located Mack's son. He is Mack's only remaining living relative and resides in a nearby Pascagoula halfway house. He has been in and out of the criminal justice system his entire life. That made him easy to find. We explained to him that his father's case had been reopened and we were following promising new leads. He was eager to supply DNA samples. This could be the break we have been looking for. Prosecution of Mack's killers may finally be potentially viable."

Also, new ways to overcome the difficulty of winning Civil Rights-era hate crime murder convictions were available, like amending charges to include "Killing on Federal Lands" or "Kidnapping Resulting in Death."

"I just want my father's name cleared. I made my peace with this long ago and stopped living with all the rage and bitterness. Now I just want him remembered as a decent man trying to stand tall and do the right thing," Mack's son said.

28

LESLEY AND CLARENCE WERE STILL working to make things right with customers Spencer had cheated. They had much work to do and had left for the dealership before sunup every day that week, working fourteen-hour days. Insurance companies had hired lawyers and investigators as well. Multiple lawsuits alleging insurance fraud were expected soon. The Mississippi Attorney General had also sent investigators to the dealership, preparing criminal charges for the arrest of Spencer. Lesley was working hard to deliver all documents required by multiple subpoenas served at the dealership by various state and federal law enforcement agencies.

"I'm deeply sorry for the unethical way Spencer ran this business. I'm saddened that the dealership took advantage of good people during difficult times," Lesley was quoted in area papers.

Lesley and Clarence noticed nothing unusual as they left Clarence's house at 4:45 a.m. The neighborhood was quiet and peaceful like all others. The moon was still visible, but the eastern sky was beginning to brighten.

"It is going to be a beautiful sunrise," Lesley said.

For George Graves, this morning started like all others. He woke early and spent twenty minutes on the toilet. He took showers three times a week and only in the evening. He brushed his teeth, then wiped his bottom with a washcloth, rinsed it out, and placed it back in the shower. Saving money on toilet paper was important to him. George peed in the washbasin because he didn't want to flush the toilet again unnecessarily. He considered not flushing as a form of personal rebellion against the federal government.

George was angry because the government regulated the amount of water each flush consumed.

"The bureaucrats won't even leave us alone in the bathroom," he protested.

He covered the official water usage information printed on the toilet bowl with white paint. George sat down for his favorite breakfast, jelly donuts and Coke. Concerned about his obese condition, his wife stopped buying donuts and soft drinks long ago, but she took a Greyhound bus to Memphis. She was visiting her sister for a week.

"When the cat's away…mice eat donuts," George said to himself as he enjoyed his third jelly donut.

Based on the new information, the FBI prepared detailed affidavits and a judge issued search warrants for George's home. The magistrate agreed that substantial evidence existed for a specific warrant authorizing the search. Meanwhile, agents had been watching George's home for a few days in unmarked cars. The warrants were sealed to protect the sensitivity of the investigation, but agents did not expect to actually arrest George, only question him. Nevertheless, they would take all necessary and reasonable precautions considering he was a registered gun owner and had purchased many high-powered rifles. He had a special gun rack built into his bedroom closet that kept his rifles and shotguns accessible and organized. Most were loaded. George hunted often and knew how to handle guns.

The legal problems George had all involved violating legal limits on game hunting. He was fined $2,000 for exceeding the six-duck limit per day, and last year he was issued a $5,000 fine for killing a spotted fawn. The bag limit on bucks was three per license year.

Mississippi game wardens claimed George killed eight in two weeks. There were no records that George ever paid any of the assessed fines, nor had he appeared in court to contest the citations.

At sunrise, police, SWAT officers, and the FBI converged on George's address in unmarked cars, an armored vehicle, and patrol cars. Four SWAT officers, dressed in tactical bulletproof vests and gear, quietly approached the front door, and three others circled around back. Unaware, George sat at the foot of his bed, putting on his shoes. The closet door was open.

First the front door was kicked in, followed by the back. "Federal agents! Federal agents!" the officers announced over and over as they moved from room to room. Red dots from their laser sights reflected off the mirror above George's dresser. Instinctively he grabbed for his favorite rifle, a bolt action .30 caliber Marlin. He thought he was being arrested for defacing his toilet or for the hunting violations; either way he was determined to teach these "game wardens" a real lesson.

He squatted behind the bed with his rifle aimed at the bedroom door.

"Come get me!" he yelled.

They tossed a nonlethal flash grenade into the bedroom, hoping to disorientate and momentarily distract George long enough to subdue him. But the split second before the grenade exploded, he covered his face with a pillow, then began firing at random. His powerful rounds easily penetrated the thin interior walls. Having no choice, the agents returned live fire.

George received a superficial in-and-out flesh wound in his right arm, and the top half of his right ear was shot off. The SWAT team did George a favor because they easily could have shot him dead. The killing would have been justified. His ear wound was bleeding profusely but was not life threatening. An FBI agent rode in the ambulance with him to the hospital.

The FBI carried out boxes of material that could be related to Mack's death. They also uncovered old KKK hoods, robes, and a Kloran, a Klan ritual book.

"What a dimwit," an agent said as he looked over the idiotic paraphernalia.

In the back of a closet was a shoebox with old photos, home movies, newspaper articles, and a handwritten note from Spencer promising to find George a good job with the city school board. In the garage they found another box containing newspaper articles about the Mack lynching and personal items that belonged to George's mother. Some of the items had mysteriously disappeared from the Poplar Grove police evidence room. The old police identification tags were still attached. It appeared George threw nothing away.

The most important evidence was sitting on a shelf in the living room, exactly where the FBI hoped to find it. A well-trained agent wearing special gloves carefully placed the small jar containing the tooth into a plastic evidence bag, sealed it, and immediately handed it to the special agent in charge. The chain of custody process was carefully documented to assure that the DNA evidence was properly collected, preserved, and transported.

A jet was waiting at the Poplar Grove airport. The tooth was transported to the FBI Laboratory at the Marine Corps Base Quantico in Quantico, Virginia. The lab enjoyed a reputation as the premiere forensics lab in the country. For the forensic technicians and experts, matching the tooth's DNA with that provided by Mack's son would be a speedy process.

In the ambulance George pled for his life. "Please don't let me die!" he said over and over. The agent promised medical attention once George answered a few questions.

"Who is the Scalper and who gave you the tooth?" The agent held a compress on George's ear to slow the bleeding.

"I'll tell you everything. Don't let me die."

"Relax. Nobody is dying. Just answer my questions."

Neighbors were concerned about what was going on and wondered what situation they were living close to. "I thought this was a quiet and safe family town, like Andy Griffith's Mayberry. I guess it is the world we live in today. I purchased my home within the last year and have never met George. Although he did seem somewhat odd," a neighbor said, explaining that she had seen George sitting on his porch talking to himself for long periods of time.

"He always wore the same clothes," she said.

29

PAVEL NAVALNY WAS A SKILLED and ruthless nego-
tiator, especially when it concerned union labor. A new pipeline he
proposed would carry Canadian oil from the Alberta Sands to Oklahoma. Richard had made the case that this new and reliable supply of
oil would finally end America's dependence on Saudi Arabia. He
appeared on both *Meet the Press* and *Face the Nation*, effectively making his case.

"American energy independence is within reach," he said.

A short while ago Richard was rotting away in one of Russell's
foul nursing homes.Now he was driving national political debates.

As a way to increase political support of the project, Richard suggested rerouting the pipeline through states with high unemploy-
ment. These governors had signed resolutions supporting it in
exchange for the job promises and guarantees. Congressmen and senators had introduced bills and spending earmarks for studies advo-
cating the use of Canadian oil supplies.

Opposition came from poorly organized environmental groups
worried about ecosystems, polluted water sources, and endangered
public health.

"Climate action—it's our obligation," dozens protested at a small
Washington rally.

But when pipeline construction began, Mr. Navalny's companies would hire thousands of highly paid union pipefitters, welders, electricians, ironworkers, painters, and operating engineers. Jobs were more important than environmental issues.

Pavel negotiated labor contracts personally and fought hard for every concession and every penny. He exploited all advantages he could find. He fought strikes with lockouts and hired strike breakers, busing them in from his other businesses. Pavel had hired permanent replacement workers on many occasions and built strong company security forces that intimidated labor organizers. His investigators had followed the wives of union presidents and used that information to blackmail them. Pavel would fire union members if they attempted to push things too far. Most union leaders tried to sign longer agreements with the Navalny companies because they didn't want to face him again.

"I would rather chew broken glass than negotiate a labor contract with Pavel Navalny," a union president confessed.

The truth was that although Mr. Navalny drove a hard bargain on labor costs, he actually respected organized labor. Once a worker completed a union apprenticeship program, she was certified and trained to do the job right. Pavel did not mind paying top wages for skilled workers; it was less expensive in the long run. In Right-to-Work states without collective bargaining agreements, workers were provided on-the-job training or they attended company-sponsored training centers. These programs were expensive and not very effective. Even the "Quick Start" vocational training programs offered in Right-to-Work states compared poorly with union skilled labor.

"I have never been disappointed with the quality of work performed by a skilled and certified union journeyman," Pavel admitted.

In recent pipeline labor negotiations, Pavel made a few specific, insignificant requests, then agreed to the union's overall contract framework as proposed. The entire process took less than two hours.

"What the hell is going on? We expected to be here fighting like cats and dogs for three weeks." The union presidents were especially surprised when Pavel brought in champagne to celebrate the new agreements.

"What am I going to do with all this extra heart medicine I brought with me?" The union leaders were very happy and relieved that everything went so well.

"There is another matter I would like to discuss with each of you," Pavel said. The union leaders took a deep breath and sat back in their chairs, anticipating trouble.

"Here it comes!" the Teamsters' president said.

"Relax, all I need is a simple personal favor." Pavel asked about the UBFGW, the United Brotherhood of Food and Grocery Workers, and explained what he had in mind.

"What does a man like you have against a small-time grocery store operator in Louisiana?" The union presidents were puzzled.

"This is a personal family matter," Mr. Navalny said.

30

JOHN WAS JUST NOW BEGINNING to feel better about things now that his financing had stabilized somewhat and credit had been temporarily restored to his grocery stores. He had no outstanding obligations with food vendors past sixty days, and a new ninety-day line of bank credit guaranteed his cash flow liquidity needs. He had completed the merger and had consolidated stores, increasing overall balance sheet strength.

But longer term survivability hinged on concessions he had negotiated with the UBFGW. He proposed taking funds from the overfunded company pension plan and cutting holiday pay. John was convinced the union membership would support demands for concessions as part of the overall reorganization because the alternative was to close stores, fire workers, and liquidate the business.

"Nobody wants to close twenty-five stores. We are confident union leadership will agree," he told a local TV interviewer. "We have them by the balls!" he bragged off the record.

UBFGW leadership reluctantly supported wage and benefits concessions in exchange for the opportunity to renegotiate contracts with John once long-term stability returned to the grocery stores.

"This generous short-term concession offer illustrates our commitment to supporting the company's financial health during this crisis." With UBFGW leadership making statements like this, John had every reason to feel confident leading up to the membership vote on the contract.

Actually, he felt too confident and had no idea the union was about to put a knife in his back. Pavel's plan would give controlling interest of the stores to the union. It would protect the workers' pensions and provide for living wages. John would face years of legal quagmires, bankruptcy, and disgrace.

A good businessperson never takes anything for granted, especially something this important. John was enjoying a steak dinner at a local steakhouse when the union membership met to vote on the new contract. "To another successful thirty-five years in the grocery business." John raised a toast with the small group of business partners around the dinner table. He had no one at the union hall looking out for his interest.

"After careful reconsideration we feel that this proposed contract is not in our best interest. The owner is making money. Workers should too! The rich drive expensive cars. What do you drive? They live on the lakefront. Where do you live? John is eating a fifty-dollar steak and drinking expensive wine right now because he thinks we are stupid and gullible. How many of you ate your dinner at the McDonald's drive-up window tonight?" Dozens of hands went up.

"Your union will not tolerate exploitation any longer." Union leadership called for a strike vote with a passionate plea to organize picket lines and walkouts.

"The fat cats should know what it's like to eat off a fast-food dollar menu every night! Let's educate them!"

Picket signs appeared everywhere; the arena looked like a political convention with everyone waving and cheering.

"Stand Together – Protect Our Pension"

"Fair Pay for Hard Work"

"Respect Our Holidays"

A young reporter and cameraperson stormed past the maitre d' and rushed to John's table. Everyone in the dining room turned to see what was going on. John's party had just finished another bottle of 1978 Domaine Leflaive Montrachet. At $3,929 per bottle, the wine was John's favorite. A security guard grabbed the reporter by the arm to pull her away. John assumed she wanted to be the first news anchor to discuss his successful union-busting strategy.

"It's okay! I'll speak with her," he said confidently.

"How do you feel about the strike vote? Are you now bankrupt?" She was persistent with hard questions as the cameraperson filmed John's reaction. "Were you really planning to raid your company's pension plans? What about the workers?"

"Strike vote! What the fuck is she talking about?" No one around John's table had an answer. Frustrated, he took the last bottle of Montrachet and smashed it against the tabletop.

"What the fuck is everyone looking at? Mind your own fucking business!" The other diners pretended to look away.

"I told you all not to trust those union sons of bitches!" He pointed fingers at everyone around his table.

The reporter told him that picket lines were already up at the largest stores. "Do you have a comment for our nightly news viewers?" she asked.

"Do I have a comment? Fuck you! How's that for a comment?"

Delivery truck drivers refused to cross the picket lines, and customers decided to shop elsewhere. The bank credit line was canceled because the stores were not generating revenue. Without cash flow John was forced to reschedule loan repayments. With no cash available and no credit, he could not restock shelves. When the loans were called, John had only one option: He placed the company in bankruptcy. The reorganization failed because the workers stayed out on strike. John did not accept responsibility for the failure.

"No good deed goes unpunished." He said he was only trying to help the union, but they bit the hand that fed them.

As promised Pavel guaranteed the new loans when the union borrowed funds to acquire the grocery store assets from Bankruptcy Court. With adequate funding the union took control of the board of directors and saved its pension plan as well. The union workers returned to their jobs with respectable pay, a strong pension plan, and reasonable holiday schedules. New deliveries and shoppers returned. The stores were restocked, cleaned, and reopened.

Much of the company's debt was tied to John personally. The bankruptcy judge refused to dismiss the obligations, forcing John into personal bankruptcy as well. He claimed $800,000 in assets and $17,000,000 in debt. He lost everything, including his house, cars, and retirement savings. John faced over two hundred individual lawsuits from retired workers, bond holders, and creditors. Many of the plaintiffs won multimillion-dollar judgments against him. John had nothing left. Even if he had money hidden away, he couldn't spend it because lawyers would reopen the litigation and seize his accounts. He bought a worn-out used car for thirty-five hundred dollars from a car lot in the town of Medicine Park, Oklahoma. He hoped the lawyers would not follow him that far.

The most troubling suit he faced was filed by his own daughters, claiming he used their trust fund for his own personal gain and made loans to himself using their funds. The Louisiana State Appeals Court held that John failed to administer the trust for the best interest of his children, and as such he was liable for the losses sustained by the trust.

John said his daughters were "ungrateful, greedy bitches."

Richard learned that a London university planned to auction off its entire collection of books, letters, speeches, and personal items that belonged to Benjamin Disraeli. "I want to purchase every item. I don't care about cost. Call off the auction." Richard wired funds the next day to cover the purchase. The items were carefully packed into eight large boxes, insured, and shipped to Poplar Grove, Mississippi. Mr. Gains had his home back and most of his furniture. He was in his favorite old leather chair, drinking single-malt scotch and reading the *Economist* magazine when the packages from England arrived. Enclosed was a short handwritten note:

"Disraeli once said, 'Nurture your mind with great thoughts; to believe in the heroic makes heroes.' Enjoy. Your friend, Richard"

31

LESLEY AND CLARENCE WERE WAITING at the Poplar Grove airport. They sat on a bench inside the only hangar. A small corporate jet owned by the Navalny companies appeared in the distance. "Here she comes," Lesley said as she excitedly hugged Clarence. They rushed outside, waiting for the plane to land. It taxied over to their location. Airport workers placed blocks against the wheels, and the pilots shut down the engines. Alexi ran down the steps into Lesley's outstretched arms.

"I'm so happy to see you!" Alexi didn't want to stop hugging Lesley. She looked in Clarence's direction. "Group hug." She motioned for Clarence to join the embrace. Alexi went on and on about how excited she was about starting college.

"Our shopping trip is going to be wonderful," she said.

Lesley was going to help decorate Alexi's dorm room and help her get everything a new freshman needed. The jet was taking them to New York, where they would spend the next three days attending Broadway plays, exploring Central Park, and shopping, shopping, and more shopping. Pavel owned a private hangar at the White Plains airport in Westchester County, about thirty miles north of New York City. A Bentley would take them straight to Bloomingdale's. They planned to stay at the Waldorf Astoria on the fabled Park Avenue.

Lesley asked Pavel if it would be okay if they took some time to visit the Grand Central Emergency Shelter. Pavel wanted Alexi to learn compassion and thought it was a wonderful idea. "I want her to have a sense of sympathy and kindness."

The shelter provided emergency housing for abused women and children in the Manhattan area. You would think a wealthy area like this would not need an emergency shelter, but on many nights desperate families were turned away because all beds were taken. Pavel gave Lesley a donation for the shelter. It was enough to cover the cost of a Thanksgiving Day dinner, provide Christmas gifts for the children, and cover utilities for a year. Lesley was not surprised by Pavel's generosity. She knew that he had probably done more to fight malaria in Africa than the World Health Organization had.

"My dad is very generous and kind. He has a big heart. But he gives secretly because he doesn't want attention," Alexi explained.

Clarence confessed, "I'm going to miss my two favorite gals."

"Don't you worry. I'm going to take good care of Lesley," Alexi assured him.

Within a few moments the jet was a small dot in the sky heading north. Clarence watched until the plane was completely gone from view. Lesley and Alexi had formed a special bond. That made Clarence happy. No one was buying cars from the dealership these days, so Clarence decided to take a few days catching up on some deferred maintenance around the house and reading a nonfiction informal history of the New Orleans underworld.

Spencer still had not shaved and now thought he looked more like Mark Twain. He also thought the new look would help him avoid the TV crews and reporters camped out on his front lawn. The disguise didn't work. Actually he just looked like a bum. The parents at Riverside Academy had demanded his resignation, and the voters of Poplar Grove had organized a recall drive. About two thousand signatures were needed on the recall petition to have a new election for mayor. After three days, over three thousand Poplar Grove registered voters had signed it.

There was a certain irony about the recall effort. Mississippi's recall law allowing for the removal of local and county officials was passed by the state legislature in the late 1950s. It was established as part of a web of strategies to limit political power of black voters. Spencer most likely worked for the law's passage. Until now it had been used only once, to recall three black members of the Claiborne County School Board.

Spencer also faced eighteen civil suits involving insurance fraud, multiple subpoenas, and dozens of depositions. The district attorney was expected to file criminal charges within the next few weeks, booking Spencer. The DA was also expected to file criminal charges separately against the dealership as well. Corporations rarely survived criminal prosecution.

The FBI special agent informed Spencer that he was a "person of interest" in a reopened murder investigation. "We need to know if you plan to leave town. Don't wander off too far," he advised.

"You're still investigating the accidental death of a black rapist! Don't you have anything better to do with your time? No one cares about some little ole murder. No one cared then and they don't now. So what's the point?" Spencer asked.

The agent informed Spencer that this investigation was a top FBI priority. "Don't go anywhere."

The Paradise Casino was a short drive from Poplar Grove and should not alarm the FBI agents following him. Spencer liked the free drinks and cheap slot machines. The casino was always crowded with gamblers, and no one recognized him or paid any attention to him. He tried to find slot machines in quiet, out-of-the-way areas where he sat alone for hours with a cupful of tokens and endless free alcohol. Twenty dollars could last all afternoon, and he usually got complimentary coupons for the dinner buffet. He wondered how everything in his life got so screwed up.

Spencer recognized a woman playing a slot machine on the next row over. He had seen her there playing the same machine many times. She seemed to spend as much time in the casino as he did. Her favorite drink was whisky and Coke, but she didn't say much and looked up only when her glass needed a refill. Spencer made his way over to say hello.

"I'm Spencer. I have seen you here before. Why do you always play the same machine?" He tried his hand at small talk.

"Because it is lucky," she said. "Once you find a good machine, you always stick with it."

She shook his hand but didn't bother to mention her name. She was extremely overweight, with bad teeth and awful body odor. Down on her luck, she was almost out of tokens.

"Do you have any extra?" she asked.

Spencer had had a lot to drink and figured what the hell. He handed her twenty dollars and ordered another round of free drinks. He had not had any female attention in a very long time and did not plan to be judgmental. Willing to overlook a lot, he pulled up the stool next to her.

"What do you have in mind?" she asked.

She said Spencer could bring her home if he liked cats. "I usually don't bring strange men to my house, but you look like you could use some entertainment." He would rather smell dirty cats than her dreadful odor. He thought the casino's garbage dumpster would smell better than her even after the free oyster and clam night.

Her trailer was about halfway between Biloxi and Poplar Grove. She didn't pay for trash pickup and piled it in the corner of her small lot. Broken glass on the front door was covered with cardboard from a cigarette carton and duct tape. She unlocked the door by reaching inside and turning the knob.

"It's not much. But it is home."

The cat smell was overwhelming. "How many cats do you have living here?" Spencer asked.

"I am not exactly sure. They come and they go."

Spencer counted at least six cats in just the first room. She explained that she used to live in a fine home near Washington, DC. "That was when I was still married. My husband made a lot of money. You may have heard of him. His name is Richard Tower."

She took Spencer's hand and led him to the bedroom. He was concerned about his ability to hold an erection under such dreadful conditions. She threw back the covers. The white bedsheet was covered with black cat hair and greenish yellow personal stains.

"Let's turn out the lights," Spencer suggested.

A short time later he was ready to go home. "I will call you," he said, heading out the door. Having secretly followed him from the casino, a local TV news crew was waiting outside the trailer, filming his exit. The photos were carried across the state and by most newspapers. "I can't get a break," Spencer complained.

32

MARK ENROLLED AS A JUNIOR majoring in social science at Tulane's School of Continuing Education. He received academic credit for the community college associate degree he had already completed. To finish an undergrad degree, he would need to complete about fourteen Tulane classes with a grade of C or better. Focusing on the individual's relationships within society, social science was considered a strong pre-law curriculum: economics, political science, and even history were included. Taking three night classes per semester, Mark hoped to graduate in less than three years. His tuition was covered by grants and scholarships.

Andre's firm hired three undergrad pre-law students each year as court runners. Mark started the next week. He would divide most of his time between Federal District Court, Civil District Court, and First City Court. Runners delivered documents and motions required by litigation. It was a great chance for Mark to learn something about the mechanics of law, and he would get to know important local judges since many filings required their signatures.

Judges scheduled certain times when they were in chambers, and a good runner would always get the necessary signatures. Most important were signed motions to dismiss. Lawyers got paid when cases were dismissed. In an average year the firm received over one hundred applications for the three coveted court runner positions.

Mark and Melissa had been looking at inexpensive apartments in the Carrolton area. Tulane University, the law firm office, and the courts were all accessible from the Carrolton streetcar line. The Carrolton area was ideal also because Pandora's snowball stand was nearby, as was City Park and the Museum of Art. Pandora's chocolate with condensed milk creation was the best in the city. Melissa stopped there every day. The University of New Orleans was also a short bike ride away.

Melissa admitted, "I always dreamed of earning a degree in English and creative writing. I want to be an author."

They found a 900-square-foot, affordable second-floor apartment in a 1930s four-plex. It had high ceilings, wood floors, real plaster walls, and it was located on the parade route. It was heated with one large natural gas heater located in the front room. "It looks just like a real fireplace," according to Mark. The small kitchen had a Roper gas stove with two burners. Melissa couldn't wait to try her hand at preparing the Creole dishes she had been reading about.

They bought secondhand appliances, including an olive green washer and dryer. Their sofa was purchased from a newspaper ad. Carpet scraps were cut to fit the rooms and used as rugs. Nearly all their other furniture came from Goodwill or other secondhand outlets. They were poor but happy.

Melissa said the Guidance Department at UNO did a wonderful job encouraging her to apply. "Many incoming freshmen are placed in remedial math and English because it builds a strong foundation for college success. Students call the program James Bond Math because the course numbers are 006 and 007. Developmental English teaches fundamentals of college writing."

Her counselor explained the process. "UNO offers two levels of remedial classes. Placement is determined by your performance on assessment exams. If you score high enough, you can also test out of the remedial requirements completely. It has happened." Melissa decided to take the placement tests that day.

"I'm a real UNO freshman! I'm a college student! I tested out of all remedial requirements!" Melissa called Mark to share the great news.

The Guidance Department said her scores were remarkable considering her weak high school record. Melissa reminded them that she held a "Boogalee degree awarded by the Camellia Grill. You should never underestimate an honorary Cajun."

"Especially not one as bright as you. Congratulations, you will do great at UNO." The Guidance Department said they were eager to follow her college success.

Mark and Melissa began to make friends at Tulane and UNO. They had a beer, pizza, and poker night in their small apartment. Mark had never played much five-card stud and seemed to lose nearly every hand. Jokingly someone around the table suggested removing an item of clothing with each losing hand. "Sounds fun, like strip poker in high school," everyone agreed.

One girl lost her shirt and bra. She tossed the items to her boyfriend. He twisted her left nipple between his thumb and forefinger.

"Cut it out." She playfully slapped his hand away.

Others lost their shoes and socks. Mark was down to his underwear, holding another bad hand. Melissa helped remove his boxers. "The rules are the rules!" she said while giving him a short, jerky tease.

Shyly Mark covered his erection with his hands. "Come on, big boy. Let's go do something about that." Melissa held out her hand and led him to the bedroom.

Most likely they would never move back to Poplar Grove. Sure, crime was a reasonable concern in New Orleans, but it was driven by economics. Urban kids stole watches or cars and moved on. "When everything goes to pay rent, my food money is spent. What am I supposed to do?" a young thief asked the Criminal Court judge.

The judge inquired about education. "I drifted in and out of the eighth grade. That's about it."

These inner-city kids had no chance. "They don't have supportive parents or any type of expectations at home. They can't finish high school, much less have any type of college-savvy guidance available to them. Young people with the most social disadvantages seem to get the least help. In the long run, it always makes more social and economic sense to build schools rather than prisons," Andre explained.

The easiest defense against street crime was to wear a cheap watch and old clothes. On the other hand, bigoted criminals like Spencer were motivated by profound hatred and prejudice. That was truly frightening.

33

US ATTORNEYS PROSECUTED CRIMINAL CASES brought by the federal government. They have wide discretion in the use of resources to further the specific priorities of each office. The US attorney for the Eastern District of Louisiana was appointed by a Democratic president. When the Republicans took over the White House, he switched parties and changed political alliances. Eager to stay employed, he aggressively prosecuted high-level state Democratic-elected officials. He won convictions against the president of the Louisiana Senate, the commissioner of administration, and the Orleans Parish district attorney. He would certainly pursue with gusto the opportunity to take down a three-term Democratic governor.

The US attorney and Andre met for coffee at the Plantation Coffee House on Canal Boulevard. It had once been a Liberty Bell grocery store but closed at about the same time that most small neighborhood New Orleans businesses closed, replaced by national chains and mundane franchises. Andre always held meetings there as his own personal protest against Starbucks stores flowering on every street corner. The first few minutes they discussed New Orleans politics; then he moved right to the point.

"Andre, did you bring the information?"

Andre opened a briefcase and handed over a large brown envelope. "Here it is. Just as I promised." The package contained information about the governor's Poplar Grove real-estate interests, Russell's Saint Ann's ownership as investigated by his staff, and the checkerboard of Poplar Grove chicanery linking it all together.

The governor bragged that he had been investigated by at least six previous grand juries, "without indictment. I don't expect a different outcome this time around." Although the governor was cavalier about the potential indictment, he had to be surprised by the number of counts. Included in the fifty-one counts, the governor was charged with conspiring to break federal racketeering laws, obstruction of justice, and bribery while improperly acquiring "several million dollars" in an illegal health-care scam linked to Mississippi real estate.

The governor was accused of conspiring with Russell to issue "certificates of need" to health-care corporations that Russell formed solely for the purpose of obtaining federal funding. The licenses were necessary before state government would authorize Medicare and Medicaid federal reimbursements to new hospitals and nursing homes. Once issued, Russell would also include a percentage of facility construction costs in patients' bills.

"Over the past three years, Russell improperly acquired fifteen certificates in the names of hospitals and nursing homes he owned. The governor then issued a moratorium that blocked the approval of any new competing Louisiana facilities," according to the US attorney's office. "The governor received about three million dollars through the health-care scheme hidden under a cloak of fraudulent real-estate transactions." He also violated federal wire-fraud and mail-fraud laws while crossing state lines by managing the scheme from Poplar Grove, Mississippi.

During his first term in office, the governor said, "Public officials indicted on charges related to their offices should be suspended without pay." Now he said, "As far as resigning, that's clearly out of the question. I have been exonerated by the greatest grand jury in the world—the people of Louisiana. They made their decision in the voting booth and I won."

He pledged to continue working as governor while the legal process ran its course, and he indicated that he would participate in his own defense, promising to address the jury at the appropriate time if necessary.

"These charges are politically motivated by incompetent Republicans."

The governor rented a room in a New Orleans hotel near the Hale Boggs Federal Building but soon became frustrated with the slow progress of the legal machinery. To make his point he borrowed a gray mule and rode it from his Canal Street hotel to the courthouse the next morning. "The mule is symbolic of the low intellect of federal prosecutors and the slow speed of these stupid proceedings," he said to reporters while wearing a top hat.

The governor was confident that he would win acquittal. However, the revelations learned during the trial would most likely destroy his political career. He enjoyed riding in the back of his Cadillac limousine, cruising LSU's sorority row. The car's license plate said "LA GOV 1." He especially liked Delta Zeta girls. When he saw a coed he liked, the driver was instructed to stop the car.

"The govna would like to say hello." The driver rolled down the dark-tinted window and invited her over.

The governor got a charge out of watching college girls undress in the back of his limo as the car circled around the LSU campus, but he never touched them. He didn't want to risk losing the North Louisiana Pentecostal vote. They did not tolerate any sexual activity outside of a monogamous heterosexual marriage. Evidently he did not take into account the same political calculus in Mississippi.

The legal proceedings also unmasked his gambling troubles. He was a regular in Atlantic City and Vegas, but he stayed away from Louisiana Indian casinos and the Mississippi coast because they were too close to home. He used aliases to hide his identity; Mr. E. Wong had visited Vegas thirty-eight times in the past year, and Mr. T. Lee had stayed in Atlantic City fifteen times over the last eighteen months. Also unexplainable were the suitcases stuffed with cash of undisclosed origin that the governor used to pay off his gambling debt.

"I am a model citizen and will continue to be a model citizen," the governor said when questioned.

Jurors failed to reach a verdict and the judge declared a mistrial. After his acquittal it was learned that one juror was the brother-in-law of a powerful Ninth Ward political boss in New Orleans. He was the only member of the jury not supporting a guilty verdict on most counts.

"I have been vindicated. How sweet it is!" the governor bragged while chewing gum and confidently rocking in his chair.

But the damage to his reputation was not repairable. The most popular slogan in the upcoming election was "Anyone Else." The governor finished third with only twenty-eight percent of the vote in the primary. It was the only time in his career that he had not finished first in a political contest. He promised revenge against all those responsible.

34

DOCTORS PATCHED UP WHAT LITTLE remained of George's ear and dressed his other injuries. He required dozens of stitches, but the bleeding did eventually stop. Half his head was shaved and covered by a large bandage that he was instructed to change on a regular basis. "You will be fine, but your hearing is permanently diminished." The doctor explained to George that he did not have enough ear left to perform reconstructive cosmetic surgery.

"I suggest just letting your hair grow longer."

George did not think the doctor was funny.

"My head hurts real bad!" George was trying to buy time.

Once he was discharged from the hospital room, his next stop was a jail cell. He was scared. George still thought the Feds cared about his hunting and the gun violations. When the agents walked back into his room, he voluntarily confessed everything he had done wrong since high school.

"We drove around at night shooting cows for target practice. We stole chickens. We didn't know anything about registering guns. Hunting licenses were too expensive, so I never bought one."

The FBI found forty-three unregistered firearms in George's house, three in his shed, and two in the El Camino. "On gun violations alone you could be looking at over a hundred-year jail sentence. Forty-eight weapons times five years each." The agent pretended to do the math out loud. "Holy crap! That's two hundred and forty years! And remember, our lab is still running all the serial numbers. I hope none of these guns were ever used in the commission of a felony. That's more time added to your stretch! We still need to consider the serious nature of your hunting violations as well. I hope you get a sympathetic judge." George was reminded that he would face trial far away in a federal courtroom with a federal judge.

"Federal judges are appointed by the President of the United States and confirmed by the United States Senate. This is not a matter for the local Poplar Grove courthouse." George was too stupid to demand a lawyer. "I wish there was some way we could help."

The agents pretended to talk amongst themselves in tones loud enough for George to overhear.

"What about those other small Poplar Grove matters we want to look into? Do you think George can help?" The agents rubbed their chins as if considering the situation. "Yes. Perhaps this could work."

"Please hep me! Please hep me! I don't want to go to jail!" George pleaded.

"If you truthfully answer a few more questions, we may be able to forget the entire gun and hunting situation." The agents pulled their chairs close to his hospital bed and began five hours of serious questioning regarding the murder of Mack Parker. "Who goes by the nickname Scalper?" was the first question.

George was cooperative and attentively answered everything. "Did I do good?" he asked. "Can I go home now?"

35

LESLEY AND CLARENCE HAD BEEN spending more and more time back in New Orleans. Lesley fell in love with the historic Creole cottages, shotguns, and Italianate mansions in the Bywater and Faubourg Marigny areas. Located between the Mississippi River, Poland Avenue, and Esplanade to the east of the French Quarter, the area is known for neighborhood bars, restaurants, jazz clubs, small playhouse theatres, art galleries, and vinyl record shops.

New Orleans flooded often when hurricanes pushed storm surge into Lake Pontchartrain, but the river had not flooded the city since the Coolidge administration. This sliver of high land along the Mississippi River attracted bohemians, artists, college students, and young urban types to its unique lifestyle offerings. Everyone got along. Lesley called this eccentric area her "sliver on the river." She was ready for change.

"Would you ever consider moving back home to New Orleans?" Lesley asked Clarence after they finished a wonderful dinner of empanadas at the Maurepas Street Food Café. Lesley did not want to stay in Poplar Grove any longer.

The restaurant was famous for its inexpensive, tasty fare made from local ingredients, and for its unusual bathrooms. Eggplant, peppers, and pork came from south Louisiana farms. The bathrooms were interesting because every other month two different artists were invited to transform them into unique art spaces. There were no restrictions on creativity, and each artist tried to outdo the others.

The ladies' room looked like a scene from Claude Monet's gardens. The floor center in the men's room appeared to be missing tiles. It was like looking straight down from the very top of the Mississippi River Bridge to busy ship traffic below. The artist created a remarkable illusion that gave Clarence a feeling of vertigo. Lesley preferred the gentle pastel colors of impressionist art. So did Clarence.

They walked along Crescent Park toward the Mudlark Theatre, their favorite place for cabaret performances. A steam riverboat was returning tourists to the uptown landing, its paddlewheel overpowering the river's current with an erotic rhythm.

"How could anyone ever leave this charming city?"

"Ten generations of my family are buried here. It's part of my soul. No matter where I go, New Orleans is home." Clarence finally admitted how deeply he missed jazz music and oyster po'boys. "It's in no way a reflection on Poplar Grove," he tried to reassure Lesley.

"I know." She suggested they contact a local real estate agent.

The FBI lab determined that the tooth's DNA taken from George's home was a positive match for Mack Parker. That evidence and George's extensive testimony helped build an incriminating case charging Spencer with federal kidnapping, conspiracy, and perhaps murder. Old home movies found in George's home showed Klan rallies with many of Poplar Grove's leading citizens of the day participating, and Spencer led the group as the Grand Wizard of the local Knights of the White Camellia. A few former Klansmen and the publisher of the town's paper were offered immunity in exchange for their testimony against Spencer. He faced sixty years in a federal prison, and the FBI was just beginning to look into other Poplar Grove incidents that were originally classified as accidents but may have been hate crimes. Of particular concern was the unusually high number of home fires in Poplar Grove's Catholic area.

Spencer had terrorized the citizens of Poplar Grove for decades and used intimidation to influence elections. But his record was perfectly clean. He had been careful never to run a stop sign or even a red light. How could he have had such an evil disposition but been careful to obey simple traffic laws? On paper he appeared to be a model citizen; that was what made him so scary.

In the 1960s it was common practice for the FBI to turn evidence over to local authorities for prosecution. Most evidence from the Mack Parker lynching had since disappeared, discarded after the local prosecutors declined to charge anyone. Mr. Gains found some, and some turned up at George's house, but recently more boxes had been discovered in plain sight in the county's evidence room.

It was learned that members of Poplar Grove's Knights of the White Camellia had unique 33/5 homemade tattoos. .. The 33 signified three times eleven. Eleven is the K's place in the alphabet. The 5 represented the modern era of the Ku Klux Klan. Spencer claimed the tattoos represented the lopsided score of a long-ago high school baseball game. "I was a great pitcher. I could also swing a bat!" he told the FBI while still maintaining a cocky, smartass attitude.

Spencer's White Camellia Klan group did not draw membership for lower classes. He recruited physicians, newspaper editors, lawyers, teachers, business owners, and elected officials. The group secretly used money and power to intimidate black and Catholic voters and political candidates they disapproved of. The group's "klabee," or treasurer, owned the town's drugstore. Poplar Groves' sheriff was the "kleagle," or membership recruiter. A local minister was the "kludd," otherwise known as the chaplain, and an elected judge was the "kligrapp," or Klan secretary.

Spencer was at the dealership alone, reviewing paperwork as required by another subpoena. Law enforcement had already seized the computers and hard drives. He'd had a difficult time finding documents since he left the administration of the dealership to Robert. He was not even sure where the warranty paper files were stored. But Spencer was not worried about civil lawsuits because his money was gone anyway, and the criminal hate crime prosecutions made his civil problems seem minor. He got sidetracked looking over personnel files. Spencer liked Clarence and respected his sales ability, but he never bothered to personally review his resume or employment application.

Of course, he didn't much like the fact that Clarence was sleeping with Lesley, but figured the marriage was on the rocks anyway. Clarence just took advantage of the situation; he could not blame any man for doing that. After all, Lesley was very attractive.

Clarence had a high school diploma and some college. He'd held various jobs over the years and lived in New Orleans his entire life until moving to Poplar Grove. "What does Lesley see in this guy? Nothing at all impressive about him! He must think he found Willy Wonka's golden ticket." Spencer was curious about their relationship but did not really care. He had nothing left to lose. "Things can't get any worse." He had recently developed a habit of talking to himself out loud.

He flipped to the next page of Clarence's employment application. On the top line Clarence had written, "Black-Mixed Race."

36

CLARENCE AND LESLEY, MARK AND Melissa—Andre's friends were all moving back to New Orleans. This called for a celebration. He was so very happy. Pavel offered to reserve Vincent's. He never did anything in a small way. Instead of reserving a private dining room, he reserved the entire restaurant. He had the chef prepare a special surprise menu. He even hired The New Orleans Swamp Gators, a Creole jazz band that did Clarence's favorite rendition of his favorite song, "Do You Know What It Means to Miss New Orleans?" The band set up in a corner off to the right.

Vincent's staff cleared out all other tables, leaving only a large round table in the center of the dining room. Richard picked up Mr. Gains. Alexi was already staying with Clarence and Lesley. Pavel flew from Houston, landing at the Lakefront airport.

"Andre, I want you to help me select something very special for Lesley." Clarence told Andre he planned to give her an engagement ring. "I want a ring with grace, history, and beauty, something with the patina of love."

"The dinner at Vincent's will be the perfect opportunity to announce a wedding. It will make for such a memorable event," Andre said.

Clarence planned to surprise Lesley with the ring while everyone was drinking champagne but before dinner was served. He wanted an engagement ring that was both unique and special, something that no one else would have. Magnificent antique jewelry turned up every so often in New Orleans, especially when wealthy families from Napoleon Avenue or Saint Charles Avenue sold to settle estates. Shops along Magazine Street were the best place in New Orleans to find antique wedding sets. The street was similar to rue du Faubourg Saint-Honoré Avenue in Paris, famous for vintage jewelry boutiques.

The best Magazine Street shop was the Mon Coeur Estate Jewelry and Gallery. They counted many of New Orleans' most prominent citizens as customers. "The gold may be worn somewhat, small repairs are evident, but the passion of life works that way. Nothing is perfect. There are always bumps and scrapes to overlook. Old rings represent the timelessness of devotion. However imperfect, love transcends generations." The salesperson was passionate about her job and understood the meaning and importance of each ring set. "Generations come and go, but love withstands it all. When our generation yields to the next, as it certainly will, this ring set will endure. It's stewardship, not ownership," she explained.

The engagement ring Clarence selected was made in New Orleans by a local jeweler sometime during the 1850s. At its center was a 1.84-carat square-cut diamond mounted on a slender band with six round-cut diamonds set along the edges. The filigree was hand engraved. The ring had survived floods, hurricanes, a civil war, and yellow fever epidemics, but somehow it endured.

"It will look beautiful on Lesley's hand," Andre assured Clarence. Clarence asked Andre to hold the ring until dinner. He wanted to be certain Lesley didn't see it before then.

They walked next door for coffee. Sitting at an outside table, Clarence said Poplar Grove was worth it because he met Lesley. "But I missed New Orleans every day," he said. Clarence was happy Lesley had fallen in love with New Orleans also. "She says it is a magical city, very sensual and timeless." They both agreed that New Orleans was always home, and they took a ride to see the old neighborhood. Nothing much had changed at all.

37

DOM PÉRIGNON WAS A BENEDICTINE monk in an Abby near Hautvillers in northeastern France. Luckily for all of us, not all monks spent their time hand-writing manuscripts. The servers opened three bottles of Dom Pérignon 1990 vintage. Pavel offered the first toast.

"To fate! I don't believe in chance or luck. I do, however, believe in fate. That is what has brought us all together. What were the chances you all would stop at the very gas station where my Alexi was sitting, scared, cold, and alone?" He raised his glass. "To destiny!"

"What if I had not accepted your lunch invitation? I was very afraid of Saint Ann's head nurse. I would still be rotting away in that dump. To good karma and predestination," Richard said. The glasses were refilled.

Mr. Gains believed the progress in solving Mack's murder after all these years was also more than just happenstance.

"God works through good people. That is why he has also brought together Clarence and Lesley. I like the way they love each other." Mr. Gains raised his glass.

"To love and happiness!"

Alexi was drinking sweet tea. "Group hug." No one needed much encouragement to express their mutual affection.

Melissa told the story about how Clarence protected her at the dealership and helped her resolve a bad marriage. "I love Mark. I love New Orleans. I love Tulane and UNO. I love my new life. Thank you, Clarence! I love you like a brother!" She gave him a hug and raised a toast to Clarence.

Mark was a little shy but also proposed a toast to Clarence. "He took me under his wing at the dealership and gave me a chance. Now I am with Melissa, studying at Tulane, and living in New Orleans. I ride a streetcar to school and work. How cool is that? I love this city and I love Melissa. Thank you, Clarence, and everyone." Mark held out his hand to shake, but instead Clarence hugged him like reunited family.

The positive impact one person could have on so many lives was remarkable.

The waiters opened more Dom Pérignon. The Swamp Gators continued playing classic Louis Armstrong and other jazz songs. Mr. Gains now believed that Mack would rest peacefully in a comfortable grave.

"After all these years Mack and his family can find peace. I had nearly lost hope, but my faith in mankind has been rekindled. To Mack Parker! May he rest at peace." He proposed another toast.

Everyone raised their glasses and echoed Mr. Gains' toast. "To Mack Parker."

Mr. Gains thanked Andre for fighting to get his home back.

"Andre, I can never repay you."

"You don't have to," he said.

The Swamp Gators played a version of "Down by the Riverside," another song made famous by Louis Armstrong. Lesley pulled

Clarence to the dance floor. "I'm going to lay down my heavy load. Down by the riverside. Yes—lay down my cares and woes. Down by the riverside. " Everyone sang along. Mark and Melissa danced in a close, slow embrace. Alexi snuck up behind Andre. "Let's dance." She had all the warmth and spirit of a charming young woman. Lesley announced that they had found the perfect house near "the sliver on the river" and would make an offer next week.

Waiters began serving the salads. "Excuse me for a moment." Clarence stepped out to Andre's car to get the ring. More Dom Pérignon was poured. The car was parked nearby on the corner of Fern Street.

"Andre, please go with Clarence to speed him up. Dinner is served. Where is he going anyway?" Lesley asked.

Clarence was beside the car on the driver's side. He was standing still but appeared to be looking toward the shadows between parked cars. "What's going on? Did you find the ring?"

Without looking in Andre's direction, Clarence motioned for him to stay back.

"Go back inside. Everything is fine."

Andre could hear stress in his voice.

"Please go back inside." Clarence was insistent that Andre stay away. But Andre thought Clarence just didn't want him to miss any of the party.

"Did you find the ring?"

Andre's unexpected appearance startled the armed man in the darkness pointing a pistol at Clarence. He was near the front of the car about five feet from where Clarence was standing. His face was disguised. Clarence had been trying to calm him down. "Take the car, my watch. I have a wallet. You can have it all."

"I did not come here for your money," the man said, disguising his voice. The area was very dark, and without realizing what was going on, Andre had stepped between the two.

The sound of a large caliber pistol fired at close range was incredibly loud. So loud in fact, it was more like something you felt rather than heard, like the big subwoofers teenagers put in their cars. It was more of a vibration than actual sound. He fired two shots. Both bullets hit Andre in the left side of his chest. The force spun him around and backward. Clarence caught him before he hit the ground. The shooter ran off down Fern Street toward the river. He tossed the gun down a storm drain.

"Somebody call an ambulance!" Clarence yelled out over and over. "Please call an ambulance!" He promised everything would be okay. "Hang in there, Andre." Clarence continued calling for help.

But Andre's chest felt warm from the blood covering his shirt. He had a strange iron taste in his mouth, and his breathing was labored. Clarence was doing everything he could to stop the bleeding without much success.

"My god, Andre, you're losing a lot of blood!"

"Don't worry. It's just one of those things." Andre didn't want Clarence to be upset. He asked him if he remembered Enos in Hynes School. Clarence said he remembered because it was the day they became friends.

"We always made a great team. Didn't we?"

"Don't close your eyes. Andre, you have to keep them open." Cradled in his arms, Clarence tried using his thumbs to keep Andre's eyelids up. Andre had trouble focusing.

"I am supposed to protect you. That's how it's always been."

"It's okay," Andre tried reassuring his best friend. "Sorry, but I have not picked out a wedding gift yet."

"You will have plenty of time for that."

But Andre knew better.

"Andre, you saved my life," Clarence said softly as he held Andre tight. Andre closed his eyes.

Dying is like falling in love; it is surprisingly easy.

38

THE *TIMES-PICAYUNE* SAID ANDRE'S death was another example of the senseless random street violence all too common in New Orleans. The New Orleans chief of police held a press conference in which he announced additional patrols in the Uptown area. "Tourists do not need to worry. New Orleans is safe," he said. The FBI was suspicious from the start. They recovered the murder weapon and determined that it had been stolen during a home robbery in Poplar Grove. Spencer was called in for questioning and named a "person of interest." He asked for a lawyer before the first question was asked. After every other question Spencer said the same thing.

"I want my lawyer!"

"Unless you are going to charge my client with something, we're leaving." Spencer's lawyer tossed his card on the interrogation table and instructed Spencer not to say another word. "We're out of here."

Highway 26 is a two-lane state road that connected Poplar Grove and Bogalusa. The towns are about twenty miles apart. A 1930s-era narrow steel bridge crossed the Pearl River just outside Bogalusa. On the Mississippi side of the river was a turnaround that passed under the bridge, a dirt road used mostly by teenagers looking for a dark place to park on date nights. Spencer had been drinking heavily all day when he decided to take a drive.

He headed east on Highway 26 and reached the Pearl River in a few minutes, tossing empty beer cans out the open car window as he sped along. Upon reaching the bridge he veered to the right onto the dirt turnaround. Spencer did not slow down. Witnesses said he was actually picking up speed as the car swerved wildly out of control, creating a huge cloud of dust in its wake before plowing into the dark waters of the Pearl River.

The river was muddy with a strong current. It was perfect for dumping bodies because recovery was unlikely. The irony of Spencer's death was that he drowned near the same location where Mack Parker's body was eventually found. Only two people attended the funeral: a smelly woman with a cat and George Graves.

Police found a short handwritten note on Spencer's kitchen table.

"I have worked hard and honest every day

Earning enduring respect along the way

Protecting our way of life, working without complaint and minimal sleep

Now tomorrow I must face sorrow and defeat

They took my dignity, poached my life's riches and bankrupted my businesses

Now rot in hell, you ungrateful bitches"

Epilogue

THE LOUISIANA GOVERNOR NEVER WON another election. Now he makes a living starring in low-budget reality TV shows. It is pathetic.

* * *

George Graves sped out of town in his hot-rod El Camino. He was carrying a small suitcase and a box of jelly donuts. No one has seen him since.

* * *

Mr. Gains lived long enough to see the Poplar Grove City Council approve a resolution changing the name of Main Street to Mack Parker Avenue. He left his beloved home "Disraeli" to Mack's son. He has cleaned up his life and enrolled as an adult nontraditional student at Pearl River College. He is interested in political office and has been encouraged to run for mayor.

* * *

Pavel funded a Tulane political science chair in Andre's honor. He has become the university's largest benefactor.

* * *

In his spare time Richard uses his remarkable talents working to promote understanding and cooperation between various economic classes. He continues working for Pavel and appears regularly on Sunday morning political talk shows.

*   *   *

Lesley's mother did not want her to marry Spencer. She realized he was not a "good man." Lesley knows it was silly to believe she could change him. Clarence is a devoted husband who loves her and cares for her deeply. Any sadness over the wasted Spencer years is overcome by her affection for Clarence.

They have used Andre's estate to establish an innovative college scholarship program for promising inner-city New Orleans kids. Clarence said that is what Andre would want. The program is special because it provides support and academic enrichment opportunities throughout the high school years.

The enrolled students meet each week with advisors and counselors to review and track progress. They are offered; tutoring sessions, summer school and time management training. The full-time counselors provide advice on goal setting, effective communications, life skills, and study habits. With the successful completion of each additional high school year, more and more college expenses not covered by financial aid are waived.

So far 121 students have successfully entered Tulane's University College. The program has become a model for other states and universities to follow. Clarence and Lesley live happily in a restored Queen Anne along the Mississippi River near Poland Avenue. Their young son is named Andre.

*   *   *

Alexi volunteered at the Grand Central Emergency Shelter every other weekend while finishing a BA degree at Yale. She attended grad school at Tulane and earned a Master of Public Health in Global Maternal and Child Health/Epidemiology, a dual-concentration advanced degree. Currently she is directing her father's African vaccine programs. She lives in Mozambique but visits New Orleans often. Alexi and Lesley remain close and stay in touch on a daily basis.

*　　*　　*

I'm proud of my husband, Mark. He is a Tulane-educated lawyer specializing in discrimination and hate crime litigation. He is the youngest partner ever at Andre's old firm, Jones, Adams and Dunbar. His mother now lives in the Villages, a retirement community in Florida. She has many friends. Mark drives a turbo-charged Jaguar coupe. He loves cars and he loves his family. We eat at the Camilla Grill often. It is our favorite lunch spot.

I earned a master's of creative writing from the University of New Orleans and love learning about this wonderful city. My first novel will be published later this year. The book is called *Comfortable Graves*. It is a narrative about two lifelong friends from New Orleans who somehow end up in Poplarville, a small Mississippi town. I changed the town's name to Poplar Grove as fiction writers do. Most likely some readers will think the book is tragic. But that would miss the point; it is not about lynchings or political corruption. It is about the remarkable capacity of devoted friendship to overcome unimaginable bigotry and positively impact many lives in the process.

A lot of good has come from Andre's shortened life. He would be pleased.

I know he is at peace in a comfortable grave.

Melissa, Honorary Boogalee

www.ingramcontent.com/pod-product-compliance
Lightning Source LLC
Chambersburg PA
CBHW051517030726

47592CB00006B/2313